... "I saw it," Marvin whispered. His voice was so low that I had to strain to hear him. "I saw the spot where your daddy died."

I watched him pick up a twig and sketch a rough outline of the crystal in the moist sand. Directly inside the outline and following the same lines, he sketched another and yet another until he had drawn seventeen crystals. His hand shook when he laid down the twig.

"That sign was carved an inch deep and four feet long from one end to the other."

He was silent for a moment and then he reached over and violently rubbed the drawing from the sand. He dusted his hands together and then rubbed his palms on the thighs of his uniform pants.

"Jackson?" His voice cracked.

"Yeah?"

"We spent all night drilling and setting up the charges for the dynamite. Come daybreak, Gordon set them off and blew half the face of the mountain into that tunnel. And you know what happened?"

"What's that?"

"When the big chunks started rolling into the tunnel, I heard the cries and screams of a thousand children. They called my name, Jackson. And they didn't stop until the tunnel was covered with a hundred tons of rock."

He cried then, the way a grown man cries, silently. His face screwed up and his body shuddered and tears cut thick courses down his ruddy face. I did the only thing a friend could do. I took him in my arms and comforted him.

Other Harmony Books
by T.K. Lebeau

The Crystal Soul Merge Series

Volume I – **THE CRYSTAL SKULL:
DESTINY'S COURIER**

Volume II – **THE CRYSTAL TUNNEL**

Coming Soon

Volume III – **THE CRYSTAL SPIRAL**

THE CRYSTAL TUNNEL

by

T. K. Lebeau

PUBLISHER'S NOTE

The Crystal Tunnel is the second book to be published in the Crystal Soul Merge Series, but should **not** be considered or read as a continuance of the time frame encompassed by the first book of the series, *The Crystal Skull: Destiny's Courier*. Each of the first three books of the series is a **complete** novel that stands by itself as a **single** literary work and all are contained within the **same time** reference points.

The relationship of *The Crystal Tunnel* to the first and third books included in the Crystal Soul Merge Series is viewed by the author in the same manner as an artist views painting a triptych: Each panel is an individual piece of art that, when viewed together, form an additional work created by the cohesive expansion of the individual parts.

Bring forth magic
Rain down fire
Create dreams
That flame desire
Call forth sunder
Laugh with pain
Restructure caring
Rename blame

Mend and meld
And flow the stream
Where flotsam jams
Get lost between
Uncovering that rusty jar
Remembering just who you are

In your dreams that drift
To you
Complacent drops
Slew mourning dew
Throughout moonlight
On the wind
Through fiery rocks
Your spire within

What you feel
Is what you are
I am you
You are my pyre
Blaze it hot
Inflame your song
Then come back in
Where you belong

I.W. Riney

Chapter One

We came to this place as do salmon to the headwaters, seeking the eternal birthing zone. We alternately soared in the skies like birds and hibernated beneath the earth's surface in series of tunnels. But, upon taking the form of men, we gradually lost our skills of communicating and interacting with nature. We forgot the ecstasy of floating through the air as a pristine snowflake. We disallowed the grace and freedom we felt as trees waving our leaves in the breeze. We shed the guileless innocence and trust that enabled us to coexist with every other aspect of being. Now, for thousands of years, we have sought the source, the interconnectedness, that vitality from which we sprang.

It was a familiar dream. One I'd had over and over for as long as I could remember. And, if the knock on the motel room door hadn't awakened me, I would have snuggled back into the comfort and nostalgia that the dreamspeaker evoked.

"Jackson Cody, wake up in there!"

For a moment, I had been back in my one bedroom trailer near the truck stop in Albuquerque and Simon Feathers had been knocking at my door, telling me to get dressed for my shift at the gas pumps. Then the heavy air and cheap deodorant of the room drifted into my nostrils and I remembered where I was.

"Just a second," I yelled at the quivering door. "Let me get my pants on!"

The man confronting me was older, heavier, and had less hair than I remembered. His starched uniform creased across the ridge where his pot belly began; the shiny badge hung over brown covered breasts that would have made a stripper proud. My eyes dropped down to the black leather holster dragging at his waist before they returned to his fading blue eyes.

"Hello, Marvin," I said, holding out my hand. "Have you come to run me out of town?"

He grabbed my hand with his right one and grasped my shoulder with his left paw. I felt the caged strength of his body. He had power, but I sensed that I was not unwelcome.

"You know better than that, Jackson. But we got to talk. While you get some clothes on, I'll run over to the cafe and get us some coffee. You got to wake up fast."

Fast, I thought, watching the door for a full minute after it had closed behind the sheriff's bulky back. Why the hurry now? Liz was already dead. According to my calculations, she should be buried today or tomorrow. Despite his stroke, Papa Gordon was a strong man. He'd already have made the arrangements, never anticipating that I might show back up. And Liz's daughter. She would be fourteen or fifteen by now. What was her name? A boy's name. Liz had named her daughter after a man. The girl's father?

Shucking off my dirty pants, I moved to the bathroom. It would take Sheriff Marvin Garland ten or twenty minutes to "politick" with the locals at the cafe and get the coffee. With a full grown beard, I had no need to shave, but the time would prove ample for an invigorating shower.

I felt the tepid spray of water on my bare shoulders and rubbed my body with the economy sized soap provided by Benson's Inn. I had sensed a feeling of urgency in my old friend Marvin that I couldn't reconcile with my memories of Bethel Bluff. Driving in last night, I hadn't observed that the sleepy town had changed that much in the last fifteen years. Had it been that long? That time, I had flown in from Los Angeles for Mama Kate's funeral; now I was here for her daughter's burial.

At the city limits, I had crossed the river and slowed for the thirty miles per hour speed limit. Acting as much from instinct as from any other motivating factor, I had braked for the sharp, poorly banked s-curve that trailed out into a straight stretch where the local law enforcers always set a speed trap on Saturday nights. Automatically slowing to pull off at the motel on the right, I had seen the red and green glare of a new neon sign ahead on the left. Remembering the state of the Bethel Bluff Motel the last time I'd been there, I had pressed the accelerator of my old Ford Galaxy and moved toward the blinking tubes ahead.

Benson Inn read the large gothic letters outlined by tubes of red gas. Next door, several cars were parked in the paved parking lot of the *Lamplighter Restaurant*. The irony of an all night cafe in a town with a population of less than five hundred pulled a little smile on my tight lips as I nosed the Galaxy into a space between a red sports car and a beat up four-wheel drive pickup.

Easing out from under the steering wheel, I closed the door behind me. Halfway to the motel office I stopped, remembering I had forgotten to lock the door, then shrugged my shoulders and continued toward the brick building. Who would break into a ten year old car to steal a worn out typewriter and a few changes of faded clothing?

I hadn't always traveled this way, I thought, pressing the bell for the night clerk. Last time I had come to Bethel Bluff in style, driving a rented luxury car and wearing tailored sports jackets and expensive leather shoes. That was before V-Day, I called it, the day I signed the divorce papers and gave Chris all future rights to my novel *Vindication*.

"What do you want?" the woman asked, peering out at me through a crack she had made by opening the door.

"I'd like a room," I answered, staring at the frizzy halo around her head.

"Come on in," she said, closing the door to pull the chain lock and then opening it again to let me in. She walked toward a counter and I watched the provacative sway of her satin covered butt. A tiny, loosely tied bow against her spine held the skimpy floral top to her ample breasts. Small wonder she had asked me what I wanted.

"Fill this out," she said, slapping an index-card sized form in front of me. "How many?"

"One," I told her, looking for the pen that should be attached to the end of a plastic spiral cord anchored to the counter.

"Just one?" she asked, her sidelong glance a mixture of disbelief and hope. "You're alone?"

I nodded and looked into the large, wide-set violet eyes hidden behind layers of mascara and charcoal colored eyeshadow. Underneath a plentiful coating of makeup, tiny lines at the corners of her eyes and lips threatened to bleed through. Twenty-five and she looked forty. This country did that to its women. She blinked her eyes and looked away.

"Here," she said, reaching her arm beneath the counter and handing me a ballpoint pen. "Last guy in here ripped off my pen."

"Thank you," I told her, as I lettered the card with the appropriate responses.

11

"Can't keep pens around here," she whined, leaning toward me. The valley between her white breasts leaked a potent spicy smell. I looked back at the form. I hadn't had a woman in weeks and this one sent out the right signals. But the thought of sleeping with someone who had to have known Liz and, at the same time knowing that Liz lay on a cold slab somewhere near, nauseated me.

"It's tough," I said, dropping the pen and reaching for my wallet. "People stick them in their pockets and never even think about it."

"Who do you work for?" she asked, picking up the card and looking at the blank space beside *"firm."*

"Myself," I said, pulling out a couple of twenties. "I'm a free-lance writer."

"Room's twenty-six dollars, counting tax. Are you a reporter?"

"No," I said, defensive about my reason for being here. "I write fiction."

"Good," she said, taking the two bills from me and opening a drawer with a key. "My boss is fed up with reporters. He had two of them run out of town today."

"Why did he do that?" I asked, watching the deep purple satin creep up the crevice between her buttocks.

"You don't know about the murders?" Money in hand, she turned and stared at me for a moment before moving back toward the counter. "We had a movie star from Hollywood killed here three days ago. Town's been filled with them magazine and newspaper reporter people."

"Oh," I said, taking the key and change from her, hoping to get to my room before she read my name and made the connection.

"What are you doing here all the way from New Mexico?"

"I'm here for a funeral," I told her, backing toward the door. The moist heat of the summer night shrouded me with its warm stickiness.

"You *are* a reporter," she accused, looking at my worn denim jeans, rumpled sports shirt and dingy canvas shoes, "but you sure don't dress like it. Tell you what. I have some cold beer in the back here…"

"Sorry," I said, stepping out the door. "I'm not a reporter. I'm a friend of the family and I have to get some rest."

"*Friend* of the family?"

She would know. She would recognize my name on the form and, by morning, only a few hours away, Papa Gordon would know that his prodigal foster son had returned.

Lukewarm water turning cold brought me back to the present and

12

I had just wrapped a white motel-issue towel around my waist when Marvin was back at the doorstep, shoving open the door with a booted toe.

"You're not dressed yet?" he fussed, setting down the two large Styrofoam cups he'd been carrying.

"I had to rinse the sticky off me," I told him, grabbing one of the cups and taking a large gulp. "I hadn't bathed since I left Albuquerque."

"Albuquerque," he mused, lowering his bulk into one of the plastic-covered chairs near the window. "We tried to find you. Wondered where you were."

"Papa Gordon knew," I said, dropping the towel and pulling on a pair of jeans. "All you had to do was ask him."

The struggle of stretching my knit shirt over my still-damp body almost caused me to miss the silence. Almost.

"Papa Gordon," I said quietly, turning to face him. "What's wrong with Papa Gordon?"

I couldn't read his face because the light was behind him. But the slump of his shoulders told me that something was dreadfully wrong.

"Gordon Anderson died two months ago," Marvin said.

"Oh, God," I said, sinking to the edge of the rumpled bed. I reached for a pillow and held it to my chest. Not Papa Gordon. The old man was too tough to die.

"Buck up, Jackson," Marvin said, his voice growing stronger. "This whole settlement is headed for hell. Things has been happening that there's no explanation for. I got feelings. Just feelings. It's like the world's ending and this thing out at the mine has just started it."

I reached for the Styrofoam cup and downed the brown liquid. Tears came to my eyes.

"Get your shoes on," he told me. "We got to go someplace else to talk. Any minute now the word's gonna get out that you're here and it'll be too late to talk."

Not a word was exchanged during the ride out to Hedges Crossing in Marvin's old four-wheel drive. I was silent in my grief, he in his fear. What type of event could have caused my old friend and confidant to fall to pieces like this? This was the man who had been wounded eleven times in the Korean War and had received numerous awards for bravery above and beyond the call of duty. This was the man who had taught me that everything had a logical explanation. Understand it, he had told me too many times to count, and you will see that there is no reason to fear it. In effect, the events happening now were beyond his understanding.

13

If he couldn't comprehend them, what could he possibly expect from me?

The tough little vehicle nudged through a thicket of young pine trees near the pavilion at the deserted campground and ploughed down a rutted road filled with nostalgia from years past. Marvin, Papa Gordon, and I had come here the last time I had been in Arkansas. We had talked about Marvin's marriage and his kids, about my highly publicized romance and marriage plans, about Mama Kate's death, about Frank's future after years in a prisoner of war camp. We had sat on large, sun-scalded rocks at a point where the river emptied into the lake; we had ventured philosophical musings into the gentle waves.

Marvin braked to a stop. He reached behind the driver's seat and dragged out an aluminum thermos. His inevitable coffee.

"Remember…" he began, large blue eyes mirroring the despair in my own.

"Yeah," I said, climbing out on my side. At that time, fifteen years ago, I could afford the luxury of being weak. The two strongest men I'd ever known had been on either side of me. Now I had to be strong; the nostalgia for that other time almost overcame me.

"Our rocks are gone," Marvin yelled over his shoulder. "The Corps of Engineers planned to fix this up for a public swimming area. They got around to moving the rocks and some brush. That's all."

I watched him gingerly place one foot in front of the other as he led the way down the steep incline to the sheltered cove. A wave of protectiveness washed over me and I questioned this feeling of nurturing I had for a man twelve years my senior who had faced more hazard and danger in one hour of his life than I had in my entire forty-two years.

"I wouldn't have recognized you on the street," Marvin said, as we scooped out places to sit on the sandy beach. "I guess I never imagined you with that rug on your face."

My feeble smile rewarded his attempt at lifting our moods. Go back, Marvin, a voice inside me whispered. Go back to those times when you were strong, brave, fearless. Go back to the times when you knew just who and where you were. I don't want to see you like this. I can't stand it.

"I grew it about five years ago," I said, scooting down onto the damp sand. "I wanted to get lost and my undisguised face was just too familiar."

"Covered up that scar real good, didn't it? When he swung that

14

garden hoe at you, old Frank didn't know that he would make you notorious!"

I fondled my chin. Even through the thick, coarse growth, I could feel the narrow cleft that had taken thirty-two stitches to close.

"I wonder if he ever learned to control his temper," I mused.

Marvin cleared his throat. I watched the muscles tighten in his round face. Finally he spoke.

"That's what everybody's wondering, Jackson. That's why I got to talk to you."

"What are you talking about, Marvin? Have you seen Frank?"

"Seen him? My friend, your brother is in jail right now, waiting arraignment. He's been accused of murdering Liz and that Hollywood actor, Jace Wright!"

Chapter Two

Often, throughout my writing career, I have used the word "stupefied." Fewer times, I have used "astounded." Some of my characters have been "shocked;" other were merely "puzzled." I knew now that I would have to find a new word that encompassed all of these frail emotions. Surely, there was something grander. An expression that could precisely describe the depth of sickness and weakness I now felt. Something that could accurately convey the feeling that the world had been pulled out from underneath my feet, that I had nothing solid to hold to.

"Frank? I thought he was in Africa, with some mercenary group."

"He was," Marvin said, "until four years ago. Then he came back home, back to the farm. He's been living in that little guest house where you two boys and your mother lived before your daddy died."

"But *why*? What happened? Frank *adored* Liz!"

"As I see it, Jackson, this is a story with a lot of paragraphs missing. Since writing is your field, you can help me patch this story together in the way it's supposed to be written. There's a word for it..."

"Editing," I interrupted. "Marvin, how could all of this happen without me knowing?"

"You got lost, remember?"

I remembered. If I hadn't written that story for *Centerpiece* magazine a couple of years ago, even Coe Wentworth couldn't have found me to offer me the contract for the story that had brought me here. Marvin seemed to be one step ahead of me.

"Just how *did* you happen to come back, *anyway*?"

Intelligent blue eyes nestled in familiar caves beneath gray dusted black eyebrows. I looked into them. Did I detect suspicion? Distrust? Even hostility?

"Marvin, believe me. If I'd had the slightest idea about Papa

Gordon, I'd have been here. My agent called me a couple of days ago with a proposition. A book publisher had offered me an advance for an account of what happened here."

"And you accepted?"

"It's not the way it sounds. First, I had only the information that Jace Wright had been killed in a freak accident. By accepting the deal, I not only earned a little extra cash, but I had the opportunity, an excuse, to come home."

"When did you find out the truth?"

"I still don't know the truth, Marvin. I picked up a newspaper yesterday in Oklahoma City. That's when I read about Liz. But, it was still being reported as an accident, not as a murder. And, there was nothing about Frank. For old times, I think you owe me an explanation."

"You're right, Jackson. You can't help if you don't know. But, remember this. I can only tell you the part of the story that I know."

I nodded. Marvin poured another cup of coffee from the metal thermos.

"You know about Gordon's stroke after you left the last time..."

"You can tell me about that later, Marvin. Let's get to the meat of this story. The last few weeks, or whatever."

"I know that it sounds crazy, Jackson, but it all started back then. Or, at least, the week after his stroke. Remember that, before her death, Kate had convinced Liz to continue at college? Well, the week after Gordon's stroke, Liz was back at the farm. She told Gordon that she had permission to graduate, sort of like voting absentee ballot. Being half paralyzed and broken with grief, Gordon let it go at that. But Liz was just sort of hollowed out, empty. And that nice young fellow that she had brought home two months before to meet Kate and Gordon? The football player? The one she was going to marry? He just disappeared from the picture. We never saw him again.

"Well, it was only a matter of weeks before it became obvious that Liz was going to be a momma. This being sixteen years ago, people didn't accept unmarried mothers like they do today. But it didn't seem to bother Liz at all. She just went on like everything was normal. She was so vacant it seemed like you could look at her from a certain angle and see right through her. Like everything inside her that was good and important had been stripped away.

"She had that baby at home in January when the ice hung three feet long from the north eaves of the house. By herself, without a doctor. Little Liz Anderson who had everything she ever wanted handed to her

17

on a silver platter. She cleaned that baby up, took the little girl in and laid her on Gordon's bed. Like it wasn't even her baby. Like she was doing a favor for someone else."

"Marvin, are you trying to tell me that Liz was crazy? That she had a baby and didn't realize it?"

"Off and on, there was times that it seemed she'd remember. She'd grab that little girl and cuddle and love her like you wouldn't believe. But mostly, the kid grew up like one of those little wolf children that you read about in psychology books."

"Feral children? But, what about Papa Gordon? Couldn't he have done something? He wouldn't have allowed anything like that to go on under his roof!"

"Gordon had suffered a stroke, much worse than you must have been told. From the day that Liz came home from college, Gordon had a live-in nurse. An English lady who did everything for him, from taking care of personal needs, like bathing and whatever, to writing letters and paying bills."

"I wondered why all of his letters were typewritten. But, if he was bedridden, why was he never at home when I called?"

"He was there, Jackson. It was his pride. He was so pleased with your book and your success. He was afraid that if you knew the shape he was in that you'd come home and give up your career."

"His speech was affected?"

"It was a bad stroke."

My head ached. The coffee I'd had earlier burned my throat. I wished for my egocentric world of two days ago, In that world, my greatest trauma had been being tricked by a woman into losing my livelihood, my pride, my self-esteem.

"What kind of childhood could this little girl have had? Why didn't somebody do something about Liz? From what you say, she must have been certifiably insane!"

"Kyanith," Marvin said, skillfully avoiding my question.

"What's that? Oh. Yeah, I remember something about the little girl having a masculine name."

"Not Kenneth," Marvin told me. "K-Y-A-N-I-T-H. Kee-a-nith. Gordon gave her the name."

"With that kind of upbringing, I wonder what she's like."

"Bright. Pretty. Healthy. Talented. And, despite it all, a fairly well-adjusted teenager."

"You have to be kidding."

18

"No, I'm not. I couldn't be more serious. If there had been any way to do it, Tillie and me would have taken her to raise. She's the same age as our youngest, Kevin. They've become fast friends over the last few years."

"How did they manage to survive all those years? Papa Gordon was well off, but even *his* finances couldn't have stood the drain of supporting four people for fifteen years.'"

"In some ways, Liz was still really sharp. In college, she studied to be an artist. You knew that. After a couple of years back at the farm, she realized that Gordon's bank account was being drained. She bought some silversmithing tools and supplies and started making big, flashy jewelry that she took to Dallas every few months and sold to them exclusive boutiques."

Marvin swished the coffee grounds around in the bottom of the metal cup he had been using. Then he slung the gritty liquid out toward the murky water. When he looked back at me, the two deep furrows in his forehead seemed to have deepened.

"Then Gordon had a heart attack," he continued. "Six weeks in coronary care put a big dent in the nest egg that Liz had saved. She started working day and night in the old fruit shed that she had converted into a workshop. About that time, Steve Benson started calling."

"Steve Benson? Alvin's son?"

"Don't get all heated up, Jackson. It was a strange thing that happened when Liz came home and had the baby. Seems that, at the same time Liz Anderson was falling down the social ladder, Steve Benson was climbing up. He went to college and got hisself a master's degree in banking, or such. Alvin Benson's roadside fruit stand was, by now, a proper grocery store and he had another brick building beside it with used furniture and tourist souvenirs. So, the county bank was pleased to hire Steve Benson. I think that Steve thought that him and Liz was on the same rung of the ladder and it was okay for him to pay court."

I had never realized that Marvin had such a deep understanding of social psychology. It seemed that I hadn't given him credit for half the intelligence and compassion he possessed. The way he related it, I could almost understand Steve Benson's rationale.

"How did she handle it?" I asked. "What did Liz do?"

"Turned him down flat, she did. Not for the reasons you might think. Liz was interested in no man. She was a cold one. Joke around town was that Kyanith came about the same way as Christ did."

"Cruel," I said, thinking of the child. "Kyanith must have been

19

teased unmercifully at school."

"No," Marvin said. He shook his head and emptied the last of the coffee from the thermos. "She never set foot inside a classroom. Liz went to Little Rock and took all the tests to teach her kid at home. Far as I know, no one ever teased Kyanith."

"What happened then?" I asked him. "Did Liz get the bills paid? God, I wish I'd known!"

"She wouldn't have taken a penny from you, Jackson. She wouldn't have taken from no one."

"I could have come back and worked the farm. I could have made the orchards and vineyards produce."

"She had the choice," Marvin argued. "Liz could have hired a farmer to prune and spray the trees, to harvest the fruit. She chose to let the orchards die. In the light of what's happened now, maybe she had a premonition."

"Why do you say that?"

"Well, if the farm had been successful, Liz wouldn't have needed the money so desperately and she wouldn't of thought about opening the Violet Fern Mine."

"The Violet Fern Mine?" I gasped. "In Heaven's name, you can't be serious! Papa Gordon would never have…"

"Gordon had no say in the matter."

I nodded. My protests clogged in my throat.

"She didn't consider the mine just then. She simply raised the price on her jewelry and started going to art shows almost every weekend, little Kyanith trailing along after her.

"It was four years ago that she got desperate. Gordon was took with pneumonia and had to have all sorts of medicines and machines. Liz had to hire a real nurse for giving shots and so forth. She went to the bank again to see about a loan. By that time, Steve Benson was president. When her loan application came up for review, Steve arranged for a personal interview. While no one knows for sure what happened, Mildred Carter, Steve's secretary, told my Tillie in confidence that Benson gave Liz the choice of marrying him or mortgaging the farm."

"She couldn't have done that," I protested. "The farm belonged to Papa Gordon!"

"After his heart attack, Gordon signed a paper that gave Liz power of attorney over his business affairs."

"And Benson knew," I said. "The bastard. He really took her rejection to heart."

20

"I think maybe Steve thought that Liz would marry him, given the choice. He could save face, kind of like that guy in your book."

"You read *Vindication*? Marvin, I didn't know you read anything that wasn't factual!"

"Plenty of information in that book, Jackson. Didn't care for the movie, but suppose it made you a bundle of money."

"It made Chris wealthy," I mumbled.

Looking off across the lake, eyes glued on two miniscule fishermen in a flat-bottomed boat, Marvin didn't seem to have heard me. It made no difference. I no longer cared that Chris knew about the pending movie contract when our marriage ended. It didn't even bother me now that she had sold the movie rights for *Vindication* for six figures. For some reason, my bitterness had faded next to the information I'd received in the last couple of days.

"Anyways," Marvin continued, turning back to me, "Liz turned Steve down again. She got her loan. Everything she asked for. Only one problem."

"What was that?"

"She had a balloon payment due September of this year. She had to come up with some big money fast."

"How did Frank fit into all of this? It seems to me that he could have worked the farm and paid off the loan."

"Your brother has changed, Jackson. He's not the wild kid who left Bethel Bluff almost twenty-five years ago, full of hate and anger. That's one of the things that makes this all so hard to understand."

I watched the waves lap up on the sandy beach at my feet. The wind had picked up and, out toward the middle of the old river bed, a frothy, choppy motion of the water told me that the crosswind had interrupted the natural current of the river. I was reminded that, even though the forces of nature seem to work against each other, it all provides for a balance in the end. When I looked back at Marvin, he smiled at me.

"Makes you wonder what kind of cross purposes we got going here in Bethel Bluff," he said, "and what it's gonna lead to."

"Did you know what I was thinking? Or, did you just guess?"

"Sometimes I know and sometimes I don't. And not with everyone. Just with certain people. I don't go around telling it. There's too many crazy things happening right now."

"You keep saying that, Marvin. What kinds of crazy things? Everything you've told me this morning follows a fairly logical sequence of cause and effect."

"That's because I haven't reached the weird things yet. I guess I've changed about as much as anyone in the past year, but it's like all those other years were just building up to this. Like this year couldn't have took place the way it did unless we had done just what we did in the fifteen years before it."

Hearing the philosophical thoughts voiced in the uneducated vernacular of my old, salt-of-the-earth friend jarred me. What had that pragmatic, stern, opinionated hero of my younger days experienced that had changed his whole outlook on life? The anxiety must have surfaced on my face.

"I know you got to be thinking that I'm just as crazy as all the rest," he said. "Maybe I am. I'll let you be the judge."

"I have no intentions of judging anyone, much less you. Go on."

"Frank had a little money when he got back here to Bethel Bluff. He used it to fix up the house some, get a new heating system, and repair the plumbing. He couldn't do too much, not in the shape he was in, so he started scratching around the mountains in the old crystal dumps, gathering up a few rocks and selling them to the tourists.

"And then the big market hit Bethel Bluff. Scattered across the world, there's people who use them crystals for healing and such. They hold them and say they can feel vibrations."

Marvin looked at me. I could sense his defensiveness, his fear of humiliation.

"I've read about the movement, Marvin. I even know people who use crystals in meditation."

"Meditation," he whispered. I watched the muscles in his shoulders relax, the tension leave his face. He continued.

"Frank sold every crystal he brought off the mountains. People were standing around, just waiting. He could of sold lots more."

"So he decided to mine the Violet Fern."

"No. Frank remembered what he'd heard of his daddy, Elmer, disappearing. He remembered the fights between Elmer and Gordon about the mine. I think Frank was like the rest of us around here. He was scared to mine the Violet Fern."

"I couldn't have done it," I admitted readily. "Even though I was only five years old when daddy disappeared, I lay in bed that night and listened to Papa Gordon and Mama, sitting on the porch swing outside the bedroom window, talking about it. It was downright spooky, hearing how Daddy had been standing there, holding a crystal, when a blue light just came down from above and consumed him. As an adult,

I know that there must have been a practical explanation, perhaps a bolt of lightning striking him. But, as a child, it was easy to believe that some supernatural entity didn't want him to be there and so destroyed him. Especially since there were other people in Bethel Bluff who could recall a similar incident years earlier."

"I saw it," Marvin whispered. His voice was so low that I had to strain to hear him. "I saw the spot where your daddy died."

I watched him pick up a twig and sketch a rough outline of a crystal in the moist sand. Directly inside the outline and following the same lines, he sketched another, and yet another until he had drawn seventeen crystals. His hand shook when he laid down the twig.

"I was a teenager when Gordon came to Pop's sawmill to get him. They let me ride along. We reached the mine in late afternoon and the sun was already playing hide and seek through the tops of the tall pine trees. A strange sort of bluish light hung over the tunnel, fading and then glowing. Gordon took us down to the opening and showed us the sign. He told Pop that this was the spot where Elmer disappeared. You know how hard quartz is, Jackson?"

"I think quartz is seven on a scale of one to ten, with diamond being the hardest."

"You're absolutely right. Dynamite and hammers can break quartz apart at the seams, but it takes a tool harder than quartz to carve it."

"That stands to reason, Marvin."

"Well, my boy, that sign I drew for you was carved on the quartz ledge where your daddy stood. It was carved an inch deep and four feet long from one end to the other."

He was silent for a moment and then he reached over and violently rubbed the drawing from the sand. He dusted his hands together and then rubbed his palms on the thighs of his uniform pants.

"Jackson?" His voice cracked.

"Yeah?"

"We spent all night drilling and setting up the charges for the dynamite. Come daybreak, Gordon set them off and blew half the face of the mountain into that tunnel. And you know what happened?"

"What's that?"

"When the big chunks started rolling into the tunnel, I heard the cries and screams of a thousand children. They called my name, Jackson. And they didn't stop until the tunnel was covered with a hundred tons of rocks."

He cried then, the way a grown man cries, silently. His face screwed

23

up and his body shuddered and tears cut thick courses down his ruddy face. I did the only thing a friend could do. I took him in my arms and comforted him.

Chapter Three

Perhaps we should have stayed there in the relative peace by the lake and completed our conversation, but Marvin had to check in with his office and serve some papers. On the way back to Bethel Bluff, I convinced him to drive off the highway and drop me at the entrance to Papa Gordon's farm. I felt the need for Papa Gordon's strength and this was as close as I could get. Marvin promised to be back to pick me up no later than three.

"There's no one around," he told me, as I stepped to the ground. "The place is deserted."

"What about Kyanith? Where is she staying?"

"No one knows," he yelled, gunning the engine. "She's not been seen since shortly after the incident."

I watched Marvin's four wheel drive lead a dusty cloud over the county road before I started down the lane to the farm. To my left, gnarled trunks and limbs reached toward the ground, Papa Gordon's prize apple orchard twenty years ago, a fray wasteland now. Sprigs of green dotted the limbs of the peach trees to my right, but no fruit was in evidence. I moved to the center of the lane to avoid briars growing out from the fences, scuffing my shoes as I eagerly searched for my first glimpse of the white farmhouse, not bothering to watch where my feet stepped.

Possessing an idyllic setting in a green, spring-fed valley, Gordon's Glen had always been a storybook home for me. Frank and I had been almost a year old when Papa Gordon had moved our mother and the two of us to the guest house. After Daddy was killed, Papa Gordon found Frank, me, and Momma rooms in the big house. He raised us as if we were his own and the farm was the only home we'd ever known, Papa Gordon the only father, and Liz the only sister.

I could see the sycamores now. Frank had planted them the summer he was ten, his retribution for almost taking off my head with a garden hoe. Papa Gordon had insisted that Frank make use of his chopping abilities and dig ten deep holes for those trees. How my brother had sweated, groaned, and complained, secretly threatening to make me pay. My job that summer had been cataloging the books in Papa Gordon's library, a task, in comparison, much larger than Frank's, but how I had eagerly worked at it, cherishing every breath I took in the leather and paper filled room.

Close enough now to see underneath the leafy sycamore branches and through the crowded trunks, I felt my heart leap to my throat and then fall to the bottom of my stomach. This *couldn't* be Papa Gordon's farm! I had been gone only fifteen years! Was this the *natural* result of fifteen years' neglect and abuse?

Even from a hundred yards away, I could detect the peeling paint, the sagging shutters, the mismatched patches of shingles on the roof. Overgrown yard shrubs and vines crept toward the house, threatening to smother it. The side of one of the doric columns caved inward. I found myself hoping that Papa Gordon's condition had been so bad that he had never realized what had happened to his beloved home.

Walking on past the house, a ghost of the past, I saw that the outbuildings were a direct reflection of the main house. One of the fruit sheds sagged toward the grape vineyard and the supervisor's office had burned. Nobody had bothered to clean up the debris and blackened stubs reached toward the sky. I felt a deep anger growing within me. Anger at Liz, anger at Frank, anger at Kyanith. Why hadn't Marvin warned me?

I was now sorry that I had come. I didn't feel close to Papa Gordon. To the contrary, I felt the most distance that there had ever been between us. It was a feeling that I didn't want to have at this point.

The cemetery lay just past the carriage house. I stopped walking. I didn't want to go and look at those overgrown graves: Momma, Daddy, Papa Gordon, Mama Kate. Then the thought paralyzed me. Had a grave been dug for Liz? Opening a grave for a family member had always been done by the healthiest surviving male. That meant Frank or me. And, obviously, I was the only candidate.

I opened the squeaking door leading to the toolshed and, after several minutes, found a bent shovel and a rusty pickax. Frank must have commandeered all of the remaining tools for his mining operation, I thought resentfully. As an afterthought, I picked up a hoe with a thick blade.

As I had feared, except for the two month old grave, the cemetery appeared not to have been touched since Papa Gordon's stroke. I bent down and stroked the red, gravelly dirt on the new mound, picking up some large stones and tossing them over the metal fence. My anger grew. Couldn't they have shown some respect for the great man? I picked up another fist-sized stone.

"Don't throw that!"

Startled, my limp fingers dropped the stone and I looked up at the stranger standing just outside the fence

"Who are you?" I asked, my voice sharp. "What are you doing here? This is family property."

"Then you must be family," the man said. He smiled professionally and held his right hand over the metal spikes. "You must be Jackson Cody. I can see that you don't remember me. I'm Steve Benson."

A cold anger washed over me. I slowly raised myself to an upright position. Eye to eye, I recognized him. I saw the whining, pimply, round-faced adolescent in this big, bland man. Blond hair had darkened brown and horn-rimmed glasses no longer rested on his nose. A good dentist had accomplished miracles with those two broken front teeth, but his cosmetic smile had no warmth. Nor would I have expected it to be anything other than cold, grim, gloating.

"You've come up in the world, haven't you, Benson. No longer a snotty-nosed kid begging for favors.

"Forget the past, Cody. We've both grown up. There's nothing to be gained now by bickering like two schoolboys."

"Don't use that patronizing tone with me, you pervert, you son-of-a-bitching, bastard pervert..."

Without my fully comprehending what I was doing, I had breached the space between us and had Benson's mottled neck in a grip between my hands. His eyes grew large and his smooth hands moved up to grasp my wrists. As if in a dream, I observed that the links in his shirt cuffs were gold. He wore a two thousand dollar watch and a three-piece expensively tailored suit. Then I relaxed. He sputtered and moved away from the fence.

"I'll get you for this, Jackson Cody," he said, backing away, stumbling over dead brush, until he was out of my sight. Then I heard the crash of his feet as he ran through the woods. Finally, I heard the powerful sound of a car engine and I dropped to my knees. What had come over me?

It had been twenty-five years ago and Frank's fight, not mine. I had found them in the draw down past the cherry orchard, fighting to the death, it had seemed. The poor girl was still tied to the fallen oak, a bandana stuffed in her mouth, her panties around her ankles and her skirt pulled up to her armpits. It had taken me only a second to assess the situation and I had picked up a pine knot from the edge of the clearing and walloped Steve Benson across the mouth. After Frank had disentangled himself, he had stood up and said, "Thanks, brother," before limping off through the woods to home, leaving me with a spiteful, senseless boy and a terrified rape victim. I cleaned up the girl and drove her home, a shack up in the hills. She never told. When I got back to the draw, Steve Benson was gone. He never told. And, I never asked Frank.

I suppose that Marvin's story earlier this morning had activated some sort of subconscious loathing I'd carried inside me all these years. And seeing Steve Benson there at that moment was just too much. I had wanted to punish him for that girl, punish him for Liz, and punish him for all the others in between. I wanted to punish him for making Papa Gordon's farm a stake in some grisly game and I wanted to punish him for being the cause of my mistrusting my own brother.

Suddenly, I'd lost any incentive I'd had earlier for digging. Telling myself I would come back in an hour or so, I brushed crumbs of dirt from the knees of my pants and pushed open the cast iron gate. Looking at the house from this angle, I could squint my eyes and imagine it as it was years ago, sparkling white with new paint, starched white muslin curtains billowing out open windows, a slender little girl running to meet me, her long, blonde braids bouncing against her back.

Desolation and depression mingled with the close summer air that threatened to suffocate me. I found myself wishing I had gone back into Bethel Bluff with Marvin. What had I expected to find here? What was left?

My eyes swept across the deserted buildings. The canning shed, tucked against a rocky outcrop, must have been the building Liz had converted to a studio. The most logical choice, the built-in, waist high tables would have provided ample space for her tools and designs. At the doorway, I hesitated, superstition laden, reluctant to disturb her possessions. Someone would have to pack up everything, I rationalized, and perhaps I could spare the pain to Kyanith.

Who are you trying to kid, I scolded myself, gingerly pushing open the door and stepping inside. You're just curious. You don't quite believe what Marvin told you about Liz this morning. You want to see for yourself what Liz has done with her life in the past fifteen years. You want to see if her work can reconcile what he told you.

I flipped the switch to the left of the door and the long line of fluorescent lights above me struggled to life. I quickly realized that Liz must have done her delicate work using the high intensity lamps scattered throughout the room.

My feet made hollow noises as I walked beside the first row of tables. Sheets of silver, silver wires, silver scraps littered the surfaces. Tanks, possibly acetylene and oxygen, leaned against the back walls. I pulled a chain cord on the long lamp in the middle of the center table and stared in surprise at some of Liz's completed work. Mostly silver, some gold, a little copper and bronze, colored gemstones, they were large garish pieces that did the same thing to my stomach that observing a Dali painting did. In no way could I connect this work with my Liz. Someone else had done it.

Memories of a teenaged Liz slipping me a carved alabaster mouse when I came home after college graduation flashed to mind. A perfectly carved mouse, intricately detailed and true to life, it foretold success for its creator. Why had she given up sculpting?

I couldn't stand it in the room any longer. I pulled the chain on the lamp and rushed to the door, leaning against the facing as I felt on the wall for the switch that controlled the overhead lights. Hot air rushed to meet my face and I breathed deeply into aching lungs. I wanted to cry but, unsure of what I'd be weeping about, I swallowed and walked down the steps.

Frank's house, the guest cottage, peeked from behind the big house. Hesitantly, I walked toward the peeling building. Even though the windows were closed, the front door stood wide open. Steve Benson, I thought angrily. What would he have been doing, poking around through Frank's belongings? The thought flashed across my mind that Steve Benson had something to do with the murders, that he must have planted evidence in Frank's cottage. Indignant, I rushed inside. And then hesitated again. How could I possibly know if anything had been moved or added? I knew as little about Frank's lifestyle as I did about a stranger's.

Sparsely furnished, every piece of furniture seemed to have a use. Sheets stretched military-like across the narrow mattress. A large trunk rested at the foot of the bed. Two chairs sat neatly across from each other at the scarred wooden table. The supervisor's cottage had provided the desk against the far wall of the living room and I recognized the swivel chair from Papa Gordon's office. With Spartan simplicity, no curtains draped the windows.

Realizing that Frank's cottage could provide me with no information, I backed out the door and looked at the big house. Despite the ninety degree heat, a shiver spread over my body. A roaring began in my ears and grew louder. I turned to look up the lane and watched, relieved, as Marvin's yellow four-wheel drive crept down the rutted trail.

"You're early," I shouted, as he stopped the truck. "I didn't expect you back so soon."

"I know," he said, laboriously climbing down from the seat. "I got both deputies to come in this afternoon and cover for me. Most of the reporters are gone and I only got one prisoner. Old Frank's not gonna give no problems. He wants to see you. You intend to go by before you leave town?"

"Yeah," I told him. I didn't know who I would see in that cell, but I already had a gnawing feeling that it wouldn't be my brother.

"Changed a lot, huh?" Marvin asked, cocking his head toward the big house.

"I didn't go in."

"Just as well. The place ain't like it used to be. I suppose you've discovered that much already."

"Steve Benson was here," I said.

"That yellow dog? He's already telling around town that the farm is his now. What did he want?"

"To gloat, more than likely," I answered, omitting telling him of my attack on the man. "He was down by the cemetery. I was cleaning off Papa Gordon's grave, preparing to dig one for Liz..."

I stopped. Shade by shade, Marvin's face paled to a sickly whitish color. He cleared his throat.

"Jackson, I meant to tell you..."

"Tell me what?"

"There won't be no grave. Those bodies are under tons of rock. We couldn't recover them."

"Oh God."

"I'm sorry, Jackson."

"I should have thought. I would have known if I'd thought about it. What about a service? Some sort of memorial for Kyanith's sake?"

"Jackson, I don't think she would come. She disappeared for a week after Gordon died. Don't you think she would have come back by now if she was concerned about any such thing?"

"I don't know. Perhaps that is the only way she can grieve. And, after all, funerals and the trappings are for the survivors."

"Guess so. Who am I to say? I never liked funerals, either."

"Marvin, I need to ask a favor of you before we go back into town."

"Sure, what do you need?"

"Well, you never told me exactly what happened. I've heard it termed *accident*, *murder*, and you even called it *incident* at one time."

"Yeah," Marvin said. "I was kind of avoiding that part, not wanting to put the blame on nobody. I wanted Frank to tell you that part."

"Weren't there any witnesses?"

"Three."

"Three?" I shouted. "Three witnesses and it can't be decided whether something was an accident or murder?"

Marvin was silent. He stood, right foot perched on the running board of his old pickup, his eyes and the upper part of his face shaded by the western hat he wore.

"I'm sorry, Marvin. Witnesses. Kyanith must have been a witness and she has disappeared. What about the other two?"

"Well, there was Moonshadow..."

"Moonshadow?" I echoed.

"Yeah, she's a hippie girl who came to Bethel Bluff about six weeks ago. She was one of them that was pressing Frank to dig more crystals."

"What does she have to say? Can't she clear up the mess? What about the third witness?"

"Moonshadow was hurt when the mine caved in. A hand-sized chunk of quartz flew out and hit her on the temple. She's in the hospital at Hot Springs, still unconscious."

He paused and scuffed his fist against the dirty yellow of the pickup door. He turned and looked at me through narrowed eyes. Then he spoke.

"Jackson, I was the third witness."

Chapter Four

"I know it's hard for you to believe," Marvin said, pouring brown aromatic liquid into the mug in front of me on the table, "that I could be there and not know."

We faced each other across the table in Frank's cottage. After his revelation, Marvin had declared his intention to get some coffee. Not yet ready to face a restaurant at Bethel Bluff, I had suggested that we make some coffee here at the farm. Frank's cabinets, as neat as the rest of his environment, yielded a scarred percolator and some stale ground coffee in a fruit jar.

"I might be able to understand if you would tell me something about what Liz and Frank were up to in the last few months, what led to the opening of the Violet Fern Mine. Marvin, do you realize that I'm just speculating that they were killed at that mine? You've talked all around it, but never confirmed the fact."

"It was the Violet Fern, alright," he said. "Couldn't of happened anywheres else."

"And?" I prodded.

"I think you ought to hear that part from Frank. I've told you everything I can. A lot went on here at the farm in the last six months. A lot I don't know about."

"Good God, Marvin! You've told me that you witnessed Liz's death! Why do you have to make this so difficult? Just tell me what you saw!"

"You won't believe me. Even Tillie didn't believe me."

"I'll sure as hell try, Marvin. I've accepted everything you've told me so far."

"But, did you *believe* it?"

"Come on, Marvin. We're friends. Would you believe me if I told you that I just saw a purple cow with five legs and that it spoke to me with a human voice?"

"No," he said, after a moment's hesitation. "But I would believe that you *thought* you saw it."

"And you'd try to understand what made me think that?"

"Yeah, I suppose so. But it was *real*, Jackson. I couldn't of dreamed up something that terrible!"

"Just tell me. I'm not going to ridicule you."

"Okay," he said, avoiding my eyes and concentrating on something past my left shoulder. "At ten o'clock Wednesday morning, the twenty-second, I ran into Oren Castleberry at the post office. He told me that he had seen Frank in Little Rock the day before and that Frank had bought some dynamite and primer cords. I kind of half-listened to him. You remember what kind of gossip Oren was."

I nodded.

"Well, he's a hundred times worse now but, even with all of these miners around here, I got to pay attention to talk about explosives. And 'specially when Frank is connected with the talk. With his past and so."

His eyes met mine. We both remembered a ten-year-old Frank constructing a primitive Molotov cocktail and throwing it at his fifth-grade teacher's house. What had the man's name been?

"Rutledge," Marvin said. "He left town at the end of that school term and we never heard anything from him again."

"You're doing it again, Marvin. You're picking up my thoughts." I watched his eyes drop to the table.

"Of course, that attempt never made it on Frank's record 'cause he was a juvenile," he said.

"You know the reason as well as I do, Marvin. You know it was because Papa Gordon sent Frank to that military school."

"Anyways, I asked Oren if he knew what Frank intended to do with the explosives. He kind of snickered and said that Frank was going to blow the ledge off above the tunnel and open up the Violet Fern Mine. At first, I didn't believe him, but then I started thinking about how secretive Liz and Frank had both been for the past couple of months. I decided to go and check it out for myself."

"Even though it wasn't actually a legal matter."

"Sometimes legality ain't what my job is about, Jackson. And, sometimes I stretch the law a bit to *prevent* trouble. Anyways, it took me almost an hour to get from the post office up to the top of Clear

Mountain. At one point, I had to pull off and go through a ditch to get around a stalled car. Liz and Frank had been driving that old jeep of Gordon's up there, but the road was still plenty rough. You can imagine how surprised I was when I crested at the clearing and saw one of them Volkswagen busses parked there, all covered with weird paintings and bumper stickers.

"I pulled my pickup over next to it and got out. There wasn't no sign of life anywheres around. I walked around the bus and looked into the pit. They must of worked on it for months, Jackson! All of them boulders and stumps that Gordon blasted into that hole over thirty-five years ago had been dragged out. The way I saw it, the mouth to that tunnel wasn't no more than two feet away!"

"How could they have done all of that without anyone knowing it was going on?" I asked.

"They must of gone at it by hand," Marvin said. "I couldn't see no big rocks. They had to have pulverized those boulders with sledgehammers and carried the chunks away. There was lots of white dust around."

I shook my head. Marvin had just described an inhuman task. As a child and a teenager, I had seen the mine several times from a distance. Liz and Frank had to have broken up and carried away tons of quartz. Even the ancient pyramid builders would have turned their backs on that job.

"Tell me about the bus, Marvin. Who did it belong to?"

"When I thought about it, I knew I'd seen it around Bethel Bluff off and on since early spring. It belonged to that hippie girl, Moonshadow. The one I told you about. The one who's in the hospital now."

"I remember."

"To get back to the story, I followed a trail around the edge of the pit and saw the two of them off at an angle and behind the mouth of the tunnel. My heart jumped up in my throat when I realized what they'd done."

"*What*, Marvin? *What* had they done?"

"They'd gone into the tunnel from the north side. Back about five feet from the old opening, they'd found a weak seam and broken through. Liz and Frank were in the Violet Fern Mine!"

"I'm with you so far, Marvin," I said, smiling my encouragement. "What's more, I believe every word."

"Well, from this point on, you're gonna have trouble," he said. "This is where it gets weird. I looked over to the right, to an old slide about five hundred feet away from the tunnel, and there stood Frank! As

34

big as life, he was yelling at the two people in the tunnel, waving at them to come out of the tunnel!"

"I thought that Frank was down in the tunnel with Liz," I interrupted.

"I thought that, at first. That shows how we're programmed, Jackson. I expected to see Frank there with Liz. But I looked at the man again, the one with Liz. He didn't look nothing like Frank. He was tall and light-haired, with big shoulders. Definitely not Frank."

"Who was it?"

"I'll get to that part in a minute. When I looked back for Frank, he was gone. I scanned the pit and couldn't find him. I turned around and looked behind me and there he was, standing there and grinning. Almost a thousand feet away from where I'd seen him not a minute earlier!"

"So, you just *thought* you saw him on the slide?"

"No, I *saw* him. I saw him on the rock slide and I saw him standing behind me. And then he was down at the tunnel. And then he was back up at the top of the mountain, standing in a grove of young pine trees. I'm telling you, Jackson, Frank was all over that place!"

"You're telling me that Frank was moving from one area to another faster than light travels? You couldn't see him move? He was at one place, disappeared, and then appeared at another?"

"I told you that you wouldn't believe me."

"It's not that I don't believe you, Marvin. I think that your time perception may be a little distorted."

"Time perception? What's *that*?"

"I'll explain later. Go on with your story."

"Well, the face of the cliff above the tunnel started sliding. I watched Liz drop something she'd been holding and reach toward those falling rocks like they was long lost loved ones. Her face lit up and she smiled real big. She never even screamed when they started piling in on her."

"What about the man in the tunnel with her?"

"He never tried to get out."

"And where was Frank while all of this was going on?"

"I told you, Jackson. He was just hopping around."

"Was he ever up by the rocks that started sliding first?"

"I don't think so."

"Did you hear any explosions?"

"I don't remember any. It was loud, real loud, what was happening

35

up there. Things was happening at lightning speed. That hippie girl whizzed past me, like she was an arrow someone shot from a bow, and hit head on with a rock tumbling down the hill. The rocks was bouncing round the bottom, filling up the pit just as easy as you'd fill a glass with water. Then them little babies started yelling for me again. They was crying and screaming my name. They remembered me from the time before..."

Marvin's voice cracked. He reached for his coffee and shakily lifted the mug to his mouth. After a moment, he continued.

"Right along then, I had stepped to the edge of the trail, ready to go rescue them infants, when I recognized the loudest voice. It was Kyanith. She was behind me, pulling me away from the ledge. Then it was just dust boiling up and loose rocks clattering down the hill.

"I looked around and Kyanith was gone, but the hippie girl was crumpled up against the front wheel of her bus, blood spurting from a wound on her head."

"And Frank? Where was he?"

"I guess he was somewhere in that hell, trying to get to the tunnel. By the time I loaded the hippie girl in my truck, he was limping along the trail toward me. We stopped at the first house on the main road and called the ambulance. When the ambulance came, I brought Frank on into Bethel Bluff and had Tillie put him in the spare bedroom."

"The guy with Liz? I take it that he was Jace Wright?"

"We didn't know that, right away. Clint McCampbell, my deputy, drove out to look at the mine and see if anything could be done as far as rescue. Remember, I told you that a car had stalled in the road?"

I nodded.

"Well, when Clint got there, a tow truck was hooking up to it and a guy in a fancy suit was yelling his head off. Turns out he was Jace Wright's business manager."

"When the car stalled," I speculated, "this man went for help and Jace went to the mine. But, why?"

"Turns out that Jace Wright was really Jason Cartwright. That name mean anything to you?"

I frowned. Something about the name rang an old bell.

"Remember the football player that Liz was going to marry?"

Then I remembered. Liz had taken him to meet her parents shortly before Mama Kate had died.

"What was he doing there? Why had he come back after all of those years?"

"I spent the whole afternoon, talking to this business manager. Luke Earl was his name and, if you ask me, I'd say he was a bodyguard, not no manager. I wasn't in shape myself to be trying to discuss anything. I guess I was in some kind of shock, numb. He said that Jace Wright had a letter from Liz, telling him that he had a daughter. He had come to talk to Liz and meet Kyanith.

"Luke and Jace had gone to the farm early that morning and had found no one there. Liz had mentioned something about the Violet Fern. Jace Wright seemed to know right where it was, so they started up the mountain. Luke insisted that the whole thing was planned. That it was premeditated murder!"

"That's why Frank was accused?"

"Luke told it that the letter was an attempt by Liz to get even for an old slight. Luke said that Liz had lured Jace to the mine and Frank was supposed to kill him. He says the plan backfired because Liz got killed, too."

"You can straighten it out, Marvin. You can tell the truth!"

"The *truth*? How many people would believe the truth? I'll tell you. A couple thousand crazies, that's who!"

"But you know that Frank didn't kill them!"

"I don't *know* nothing, Jackson. I can't clear nobody."

I found myself wondering whether I would have the guts to repeat a story like Marvin's if I had experienced it. Even to a trusted friend. Marvin Garland still had to be the bravest man I'd ever known.

37

Chapter Five

The county jail, located on the courthouse square at Bethel Bluff, was new, constructed sometime during the years I'd been gone. The old jail, a cramped, native stone oven, peeped from behind and to the right of the more modern concrete and glass structure. I could hear the blood rushing in my ears, corresponding to the increased beat of my heart. Antipathy crept over me. Did I really want to see Frank? Could I reconcile the Frank of my youth with what he must have become?

Summer heat had warmed the asphalt and I picked my way over shiny patches of black on the sidewalk. Marvin led the way and I followed, mesmerized by the sway of his hips, the leading movements of his shoulders. He paused at the plate glass door and turned to face me.

"He's not the same, Jackson. Frank has changed more than any of us except…"

He paused for a moment and I finished his sentence.

"Except Liz."

"Yeah."

"I have to do it, Marvin. For Frank *and* for me."

We passed a desk guarded by a pleasant-faced graying woman in beige and paisley. Using a key on the ring attached to one of his belt loops, Marvin opened a dark green metal door and I stepped through the opening. The door closed behind me and I heard the clicks and thuds that locked us in the cellblock, prisoners with Frank.

"He's in the last cell to your right," Marvin said, brushing past me and leading the way. He glanced at me and I sensed an apology in his look. "Tillie tried to make him comfortable. She sent some quilts and blankets from home."

The cell was dark and I stared through the spaces between the shiny metal bars, toward the shadowed corner where my brother lay. Despite the summer heat, bulky layers of covering hid his body. As my eyes

grew accustomed to the dimness, my searching gaze stopped, paralyzed, when I saw the darker object leaning against the wall.

"What's that?" I whispered, pointing to the squatty dark object
attached to a black, high-topped shoe.

Marvin shook his head, clearing it of some invisible annoyance,
and inserted a key in the square box attached to the metal bars. He turned
it before he looked at me.

"That's an artificial leg, Jackson. It belongs to Frank."

He swung the cell door open and I followed him in, eyes fixated on
the bed. The covers moved and I watched my brother scoot himself to
an upright position and then lean back against the wall.

"That you, Jackson?"

I swallowed, trying to dislodge the lump that had formed in my
throat. Moving forward, I held out my right hand to the stranger. He
grasped it with his left hand and I felt his cool, bony fingers pinch the
flesh of my hand.

"I knew you'd come. I told Marvin that you would. 'Jackson's
smart,' I told him. 'He can straighten up just about any mess.'"

I felt the lump growing in my throat again as I tried to pull my hand
away from Frank's. His grip tightened, forcing me to remember his
years of physical training in the special forces and then as a mercenary.

"I would have thought that you could have handled anything,
Franklin." My voice came out higher, thinner than I had wanted.

He chuckled then, a rattly sound that broke off into a cough. I
squinted, trying to find something in that thin, drawn face that coincided
with my memories. If I could see his eyes, black and snapping, filled
with anger, remorse, or glee, I would know that this frail bundle of flesh
was Frank. But deep hollows shadowed his eyes and his high cheekbones, devoid now of excess flesh, served to further camouflage his
identity. He relaxed his grip and I pulled away my hand, brushing my
moist palm on my denim pants.

"I was fairly good at making the messes, brother. But you took care
of the clean-up work. You're the one who always made it right."

"I don't know about that."

Frank snorted. Marvin shifted his weight from one foot to the other.
Then he reached into a corner and pulled out a folding chair.

"Here, Jackson," he said, shoving it toward me. "You and Frank
visit a spell. I'll be back in a couple of hours."

I felt the flesh on my head draw as Marvin closed the cell door. Even
as children, Frank and I had never found more than ten minutes worth

39

of mutual conversation.

"It'll take two hours," Marvin said, from outside the cell. "Believe me, you'll need that much time."

He had done it again. He had picked up my thoughts.

***

It hadn't taken Frank and me long to cover the first twenty years of our twenty-five years' separation. After being MIA from 1964 to 1968, Frank had come back to Bethel Bluff upon his discharge. Within a month, he had re-enlisted and left again for Vietnam. In 1973, he was again back in Bethel Bluff for a week or so before he left for Africa, hired by a mercenary group. He was there for seven years before he finally came home.

"You lost your leg in Africa?" I asked him.

"Yeah," he said. His stare fell to the spot on the bed where the covers should have been mounded by his right calf and foot. "That's a mistake I'll never make again. Tribal retribution."

"You were captured by natives?"

"Hell, Jackson! How can you be so dense and still succeed at writing? I was messing around with one of the villagers!"

"And they cut off your leg?"

"My punishment was mild. They cut off his male organ and left him strung up for the birds to eat."

The lump was back in my throat. My entire head seemed to pound with the beat of my heart.

"*Him?*"

"Now, don't tell me that you didn't *know*."

"Good God, Frank! I had no idea! I had even speculated that you and Liz might have..." My voice trailed off as I realized fully the implications of what he had told me. "But *when? How?*"

Frank chuckled again, a laugh with no mirth. He pulled his body straighter on the bed and leaned back. His head made a thudding sound as it bounced against the wall.

"Remember fifth grade, Jackson? The year that I really started getting in trouble? The year that I had to stay after school day after day, week after week?"

I nodded.

"Did you really think that I was doing book work all those hours?" Frank sat up abruptly and then leaned back against the wall. "If that had been the case, I would of been pretty smart, huh? I wouldn't of had to repeat the fifth grade, would I?"

I remembered Frank's unreasonable anger after he had discovered he was being retained. I remembered trying to tell him that repeating the fifth grade would make almost no difference over the entire scope of his life. I remembered his anger with me. I remembered the bomb he had thrown at his teacher's house. Now, I understood.

"Why didn't you tell me, Frank? I could have helped!"

"How could you have helped me? Told the whole town that Rutledge was a fag and that he was using me as his pretty boy? I had a reputation as a tough guy, Jackson. I couldn't have allowed that to happen. Besides, at *that* point, I still had a chance."

"So you chose to be labelled as incorrigible and violent."

"It was better than being called *queer*."

"You said you had a chance at that point. What happened?"

"Well, as I said earlier, Jackson, you've always managed to make things right. You talked Papa Gordon into getting me to the military school. That saved me from going to reform school."

"And?"

"Well, it was like I was wearing a label, Jackson. Like these older guys *knew*. It wasn't long before I found out that the only way I could make it at that military school was to whore my way through."

"God, Frank!"

"After awhile, it wasn't so bad. When I could choose my partner, I enjoyed it. And, even later, it was the only way. I never could make it with a woman."

"But you were so *macho*! Always talking about your sexual exploits with women. *Many* women."

"That was part of the game, Jackson."

"I still wish you would have told me."

"No, you don't," Frank said. "Even now, you wish that you didn't know And then you wouldn't feel guilty."

"Maybe."

"Well, don't feel guilt," he said. "At any point, I had a choice. I just chose wrong according to society's standards."

I couldn't think of an appropriate response. There *was* none.

"I came back to Bethel Bluff four years ago," Frank continued. "I had plans to help Papa Gordon with the orchards and just hide out at Gordon's Glen until I died."

"But you, like me, had no idea of how sick Papa Gordon was, how the farm had deteriorated."

"I never would have imagined it could be that bad," he said. "It took

41

most of the money I had stashed away just to fix up the guest house and repair the roof on the main house. You saw it? Marvin said you went out there."

I nodded.

"One day, I wandered up on Beaver Mountain. Not a small task when you consider I had *that* thing strapped to me." He pointed to the prosthesis leaning against the cell wall. He grinned and I saw a ghost of the old Frank. "Well, I ran across a ditch where one of the old crystal miners had dumped some tailings and I picked up some of the crystals that had washed out of the mud. I stopped by the Bluff Cafe on the way home and showed them to Shorty Milner, who's running the place now. A tourist offered me five dollars for them. All I had to do was to go to one of those old prospecting holes every day and pick up a handful of crystals. The rest is history."

"You don't get off that easy, Frank You haven't said one thing about Liz or the Violet Fern."

He flinched, almost as if he had been slapped. Then he scooted toward me and I finally saw his eyes. Sunken into his skull, they blazed alternately with fear and defensiveness, an expression similar to Marvin's earlier one.

"There's not much to say about Liz. She just wasn't Liz. Matter of fact, she wasn't nobody. She was just an empty shell that looked like Liz."

"Marvin told me almost the same thing."

"Everyone knew. All you had to do was to be around her for five minutes. Remember how much fun she used to be, joking and laughing?"

I nodded.

"And how sweet and loving she was?"

"I remember."

"It was like someone used a big straw and sucked all of those good things out of her, Jackson. She didn't become bad. She just turned into a plastic doll."

"Do you think she was sick? Mentally, I mean?"

"Everyone's crazy, Jackson. It's just a question of how much. I don't know as Liz was any crazier than the rest of us."

"I'm no psychiatrist, Frank. But you and Marvin have both told me that Liz's behavior was not normal."

"You don't understand," he protested. "She didn't do crazy things. She just didn't do nothing that had any feelings."

"Example, Frank. Give me an example."

"Well, take the time that Kyanith carved the mouse out of a thick piece of shale. Happened a couple of years ago. Bear in mind that this little girl has been making animals out of rocks most of her life, a lot of them better than that mouse, and I never saw Liz make a fuss over any of them. Sometimes, she would nod when Kyanith would show her a piece. Sometimes, she just ignored her.

"But the mouse must of been special because she took one look at that little creature nestled in Kyanith's palm and her face lit up like someone had turned on a lamp inside her. She folded Kyanith up in her arms and started laughing and crying at the same time, telling Kyanith over and over how much she loved her. She told Kyanith that the mouse showed traces of Andy's talent."

"Who is Andy?"

"I don't know," Frank admitted. "I thought that *you* might."

"What made you think that?"

"Well, it seems that Andy was one of Liz's two best friends that she made while she was in college. Andy and Betsy was their names. Every so often, she mentioned one of them. I guess you'll have to ask Kyanith about them. She's a smart little girl."

"When Liz was a kid, she carved me a little mouse," I mused. "I've often wondered why she didn't continue sculpting. She had tremendous talent."

"That's what her friend, Andy, did," Frank said. "She's a famous artist in New York City. Besides, Liz had to come home and take care of Papa Gordon."

"Were you ever able to communicate with Papa Gordon?" I asked, changing the subject. I didn't want to hear any more about the Liz that Frank described.

"After a fashion," he said. "By the time she was six or seven, Kyanith had developed a kind of finger signal talk with Papa. They would sit for hours, wiggling their fingers at each other. She was a translator for me."

"What did he think about what had happened to Liz?"

"I never asked him. The time that he had with Kyanith was the only good he had left. And it was the only time I ever heard Kyanith laugh. It just didn't seem right to bring up unpleasant things."

"I see."

"Come on, Jackson. Ask me. I know you've been dying to find out about the Violet Fern."

"You're right, Frank. Surely you remember what happened to Daddy. We grew up with Papa Gordon telling us how dangerous it was. Did you forget? Or did you think he was just a crazy old man?"

"It's more complicated than that, Jackson. It wasn't a matter of memory. And, as for Papa Gordon, I believed every word he ever told me. I still do."

"Then why, in the name of God, did you do it?"

"I suppose Marvin told you that Liz mortgaged the farm."

"He did."

"She didn't tell Papa Gordon. She was making the yearly payments just fine. But she had a big payment coming up this fall."

"A balloon. Marvin told me about that, too."

"It seems like he told you everything, Jackson. Why are you making me go over it again?"

"He didn't tell me why you opened the Violet Fern Mine. *Why* Frank? There are other mines around!"

Frank's body slumped for a moment. He shook his head.

"Marvin didn't tell you how much the balloon payment was?"

In turn, I shook my head and leaned forward. My ears strained as he continued.

"Picking up those crystals out of the old dumps, I could make five bucks on a bad day, fifty on a good one. Figure it out, Jackson. There was no way I could make seventy-five thousand in time for that payment."

"Good God."

"Steve Benson wanted the farm," Frank said. "Or Liz. The only chance he had was to make easy yearly payments and then one big hunk that he knew she couldn't come up with."

Again, I felt the anger threatening to surface and I breathed deeply. Frank sat up straighter.

"Early this spring a girl came to town. She stayed around awhile and heard some of the stories about the Violet Fern. She came to me and asked me a bunch of questions about phantoms and tabulars."

"You're going to have to give me a refresher course on quartz crystals," I told him. "I've been away a long time."

"Tabulars are the flat ones," Frank said. "The ones that have six sides like all quartz crystals, but four of the sides are so skinny that sometimes you have to find a couple of them with a magnifying glass or a microscope."

"I remember now. And phantoms are like a perfectly developed

44

crystal inside another crystal. A ghost crystal."

"Usually colored blue or black by manganese," Frank continued. "Occasionally, chlorine colors the phantom green or a brownish one is colored by iron. What's wrong with you?"

I shook my head, not trusting my voice. This discussion had become an uncomfortable reminder of the hallucination Marvin had experienced when Papa Gordon had caved the cliff onto the tunnel opening almost forty years ago.

"That girl, Moonshadow, offered a lot of money for some of those crystals, Jackson. Enough to make that bank payment."

"Unless my memory fails me, phantoms and tabulars have been found in almost every crystal mine around. I still see no justification for opening the Violet Fern."

"You don't understand what I'm saying, Jackson. I don't know how she did it, but she must of seen Papa Gordon's crystal. You don't remember it?"

"No, I don't."

"He kept it in a lead box in his safe. I only saw it once. Right before I joined the Marines."

"A lead box?"

"Yeah. Like it was radioactive."

"Crystals don't give off harmful radiation."

"I know that, Jackson. But this crystal was different from any I'd ever seen."

"How was it different?"

"I can't talk much longer, brother. I'm getting awfully weak."

"Okay, Frank. I'll come back tomorrow. Marvin must be back by now."

"Kyanith can tell you," he said, his voice trailing into a whisper. "She'll be up at the cabin by the mine."

I stood up and bent over the bed, pulling Frank to a reclining position and laying his head on the pillow. He reached up and placed a shaking hand on my cheek.

"It was a tabular, Jackson. Flat as a piece of paper and it had seventeen chevrons lined up in it."

He closed his eyes. I felt waves of cold waft over my body. He had described Marvin's sand drawing perfectly. Had they discussed this? Or, had both men independently had similiar experiences?

45

Chapter Six

I stirred the soggy vegetables with a fork. Succotash, the menu had read, but the chef at the Lamplighter Restaurant had most likely studied gourmet cooking right here in Bethel Bluff. I moved my fork over to the slaw. It was palatable and I concentrated my attention on eating it, realizing that I hadn't ingested anything solid since the day before yesterday. Small wonder that I'd found myself suffering bouts of anxiety, frustration, and depression. When Marvin had dropped me off at the room thirty minutes ago, I'd come right over here to eat.

"Mr. Cody? Jackson Cody?"

Startled, I raised my head and looked at the woman sitting opposite me. I hadn't even seen her sit down at the booth. If the bandage on her forehead hadn't clued me to her identity, her sixties flower-child garb would have.

"I'm Jackson Cody. You must be Moonshadow."

"Katharine Allison," she said, extending her right hand across the table. "We've met before. At a party at my parents' home in the sixties. You wouldn't remember me. I was a homely twelve and you had a beautiful blonde actress clinging to your arm."

"I'm sorry," I stuttered, touching her hand briefly. Allison. Of course. Katharine Allison's kidnapping would have been the news story of the decade had not Patty Hearst been kidnapped the same week. Katharine's plight had never made it to the front page.

"I can see by your frown that you're remembering," she continued. "Admittedly, it was not the nicest thing to do to my parents, but they weren't very nice to me, either. And the interest on the ransom money has provided for me since then."

"It was a *hoax*? But they found your body!"

"They found the badly burned body of a poor young thing who took too many drugs. With my driver's license, naturally. In their eagerness to cut their losses, my parents made a positive identification of the body and no further tests were needed."

"So you took her identity."

She shook her head and a distant look came to her hazel eyes. Then she spoke.

"You remember Haight-Ashbury, Mr. Cody. That poor girl could easily have been just like me, an unwanted offspring of rich parents. It would have been too risky to assume her identity. I created a new one."

"A *new* identity?"

"It's amazing what a little money in the right hands can accomplish."

"So you scorned and rejected your parents' materialistic way of life and yet you've lived off their money all of these years."

She shrugged. A limp strand of gray-streaked blonde hair crawled over the bandage on her forehead. When she pushed it back, I realized that her long fingers trembled and her nails were bitten to the quick.

"I've earned my way, Mr. Cody. I've worked for everything that I've gotten. But, in a sense, you're right. I had intended to use that money to buy some special crystals from your brother."

"The phantom tabulars."

Her thin lips tightened and her mouth pulled up in a bitter smile. She chuckled grimly.

"You've talked to either Frank or Kyanith."

I nodded.

"I suppose you're wondering why I would offer a hundred thousand dollars for a few crystals."

"I don't see that it's my place to worry about how or why you spend your money. I've foolishly given away hundreds of thousands of dollars myself."

"I heard about the movie made from your book. It came so soon on the heels of your divorce that I figured you must have made that a part of your settlement."

I picked up one of the rolls at the side of my plate and debated smearing margarine on it. Pinching off a bit of the crust, I stuck it in my mouth.

"Mr. Cody?"

"Please. Just call me Jackson."

"I feel the need to explain this to you. Three years ago, I began channeling."

"Channeling?" What could she be talking about? Was this some new type of swimming? A boating marathon? What did it have to do with her desire for the crystals?

"Channeling is a psychic process whereby I become the vessel for a higher entity to communicate."

"You mean that you're a medium? That you get messages from the dead? Trances, seances, and the whole bit?"

"It's not as extraordinary and occult as you seem to think, Jackson. More and more people are discovering that they have this ability."

"Why am I feeling a desire to terminate this conversation?"

"Because you're afraid of the truth."

"Come on, now, Katharine, or Moonshadow, or whatever you call yourself. I don't have time to sit here and listen to you telling me that some dead Indian told you to come to Arkansas and tempt my brother to open a dangerous mine!"

"Hr...umph," I heard the voice and looked at the person standing at my left. She spoke. "Do you want some more coffee?"

I nodded and the waitress sloshed some brown liquid into the thick cup. I scooted my plate to the edge of the table and she picked it up.

"Okay," I said, after she left. I looked back at Moonshadow and lowered my voice. "Tell the story your way. I'll try not to interrupt."

"First of all, Jackson, your conception of death is all wrong. These aren't dead people who communicate through me. They're just at another level, having completed their assignments at this level. They're not really dead, because there is no past or present. We don't live linear lives. Everything is happening at this one moment..."

She stopped. The expression on my face must have conveyed my disbelief and alienation.

"Oh, I'm not doing a very good job of explaining this," she said. "You have to sort of grow into the concept and I sense you're not ready."

I continued staring at her. Picking up my spoon, I lifted a cube of ice from my water glass and dropped it into my coffee. I decided that I would allow her five more minutes.

"Let me start with last December," she pleaded. "This won't take long. You don't have to *believe* me. Just *hear* me."

"Okay," I said, sipping the coffee. It was still too hot and I reached for my spoon.

"A friend and I were in Boulder, Colorado, snowed in. For lack of anything better to do, we began experimenting with a Ouija board we had found in a closet. Immediately, I began receiving messages from an entity called Harmony."

48

Harmony, I thought, sipping the now-cooled coffee. How corny. How flower-child stupid! If I sipped the coffee slowly, it would last me another four minutes.

"Harmony is a group of souls," she continued. "Some of them have passed over and some are still living on this plane. They chose, in this life, to work toward achieving peace and harmony in the world..."

Moonshadow must have become aware of my reluctance to hear more, my impatience to leave. She began speaking quickly, softly.

"The Harmony soul group cannot achieve its purpose without the cooperation of still another soul group, a soul group that can recover the hidden secrets needed by Harmony."

"So, you're part of this second soul group and the secrets are hidden in the crystals from the Violet Fern Mine."

I couldn't resist the tongue-in-cheek conclusion, but I was completely unprepared for Moonshadow's reaction. Her face seemed to take on length, her cheekbones became more prominent, and her eyes darkened. When she spoke, it was with a deep, heavily accented voice.

"You are not as far from the truth as you might think, my friend."

"What the *hell*" I yelled, flattening my body against the back of the booth, shrinking from the thing across the table from me. A thought brushed my mind: Would I be able to tell Marvin about this experience?

* * *

I shook for a full thirty minutes after my mad exit from the restaurant and departure from Moonshadow. Marvin had been right. This whole part of the country was crazy, falling apart. I had watched a woman's facial characteristics change. I had heard her speak to me with a masculine voice. But, even more, the frightening aspect, was the fact that, somewhere within me, the voice had resonated. I had recognized the voice. I had *known* the voice.

Totally unprepared for the light tap on the motel door, I flinched and almost slipped off the edge of the bed where I had been sitting. My mind protested that I couldn't assimilate another piece of information. I *had* to rest. But the knocking persisted and I dragged myself to a standing position and jerked open the door. The motel clerk stood there, a liquor bottle in one of her hands and some paper cups in the other.

"I thought you might need this," she said, sliding past me into the room. "Lorelle, the waitress at the Lamplighter, said you looked pretty awful after you talked to that hippie girl."

"I suppose I did," I said, watching her shove a book to the side and place the bourbon on the plastic table by the window. "But I don't need that liquor. After my experiences today, I'd probably get depressed."

"Oh, you won't do that," she smiled, a secretive little grimace. "I won't let you."

"Uh…"

"I'm not on duty tonight," she said, sitting down in the chair nearest the wall. "I'm staying with you."

* * *

It was almost dawn before she emptied the bottle. I had nursed my first drink for a couple of hours and, after that, she hadn't bothered to ask me if I wanted another. Yet, I can't say that I've ever seen anyone so coldly sober. There was a tightness in her, a rigidity that belied the tranquilizing effects of the alcohol.

"What's your name? I asked her.

She breathed deeply and then poured the liquid from the paper cup into her mouth. I watched her throat work as she swallowed. She shook her blond hair back from her face and fiddled with a button on the cuff of her plaid western-cut shirt.

"Dorothy," she said, her voice so low that I had to strain to hear it. "But most everybody calls me Dorrie."

"Dorrie," I repeated, reaching over and cradling her right hand in my left one. "It's a nice name. And you're a nice girl, Dorrie."

She turned to me, gray dawn illuminating the surprised expression on her face. I watched it change to disbelief and then anger. She stood up, jerking her hand away from mine.

"Don't make fun of me," she whispered.

"I'm not!" I said, standing up and grabbing her wrists. "I really mean it. I like you!"

"I told you all about me,"she said angrily, loosening my grip on her wrist with her free hand. "I'm not fit for you to like. I'm bad!"

"No, you're not," I said, squeezing her wrists. She flinched and I remembered the scars and bruises on her wrists. I loosened my grip. "I'm sorry, Dorrie. I didn't mean to hurt you. The man who did that to you. Is he the one who told you that you were no good?"

She nodded, rubbing her wrist. I could see the left side of her face now and I watched a shiny streak of liquid creep down her cheek.

"Come on," I said, pulling her to me and hugging her. "It's okay to cry. Just don't believe that you're bad because one man told you that. He has to be crazy, anyway, to hurt you like that. Forget him and what he told you."

"I can't," she whispered, pressing her forehead to my shoulder.

50

I felt warm liquid seep through the fabric of my shirt and trickle down my chest.

"Yes, you can," I said sternly. "There are other men in the world. Good men. You're an attractive woman and you have a heart. You don't have to tolerate someone who feels the need to hurt you in order to prove he's a man."

She looked up at me, still sniffling. I pulled up my shirt tail and wiped the moisture from her cheeks. Moving away from me, she sat down in the vinyl upholstered chair next to the window. In the light of pale dawn, I could see her slumped profile.

"I was fifteen years old when he came and took me away," she said. "He gave my daddy some money for liquor and took me with him."

"Your father *sold* you?" I gasped, dropping back to my chair. "He sold you to a *sadist*?"

"Except for the sex stuff, it wasn't much different from being at home. And, except for nights, it was a whole lot better, because he bought me nice clothes and gave me my own room to live in here at his motel."

"I still find it hard to believe that something like that could happen in this day and time. What did your mother say about it?"

"She died when I was thirteen," Dorrie said quietly. "But she was always good to me."

We sat silently for several seconds. Then Dorrie cleared her throat.

"She was in love with you."

"W*hat*?"

"My mother used to tell me about you. She said that you were like a prince in a fairy tale. She said that you were a gentleman and you really cared about people."

"I didn't even k*now* your Mother!"

"You just forgot," Dorrie said. "You were important and she was nobody."

I remained silent.

"When she was fifteen, she was raped," Dorrie said. "Mama told me that the guy who did it would have killed her, but you came along and saved her."

An image of a frightened girl tied to a tree twenty-five years ago flashed through my mind. I remembered how Steve Benson's neck had felt yesterday. Nausea wrenched through my body.

"Dorrie?"

"Yeah."

"The man that you call Daddy, was he your real father?"

"No," she whispered. "The man who raped mama was my real father."

"Did your mother ever tell you the name of the man who raped her?"

"No. I don't think she knew. his name."

I stood by the window and watched her walk across the parking lot. Behind her, the red neon letters alternately flashed off and on. *Benson's Inn*. Blackness. *Benson's Inn*. Blackness. I waited until she reached the door of her room next to the motel office before I dragged myself to the bathroom and vomited.

Chapter Seven

By the time I reached his cell, Frank was sitting up on the edge of his cot, fully dressed in khakis and scraping the last bite of food from a metal plate. The door to his cell was open and, when he saw me, he grinned.

"I'm a free man, Jackson. They're letting me go. About eight this morning, that Moonshadow came in and gave a statement that cleared me."

"Wonderful," I said, hoping I sounded cheerful. "Are you going back to the farm? I'll drive you."

"I'm not going to the farm," Frank said, wiping his mouth with the back of his right hand. "Marvin told me he would take me up to the mine."

"To the Violet Fern? *Why?*"

"I have to find Kyanith. Make sure she's all right."

I had forgotten about Kyanith. I also needed to talk to her. Perhaps a teenager would have a more realistic account of those moments at the Violet Fern just before the slide.

"Where is Marvin?" I asked Frank. "He wasn't in the office when I came through."

"More than likely, he's over at the Bluff Cafe, having a cup of coffee. You can go over and tell him that I'm ready to go."

Already, he was sounding more like the old Frank. I felt my spirits lift. I could tolerate bossiness, arrogance and dogmatism more easily than helpless requests and apologies from yesterday's withdrawn creature.

"Well, what are we waiting for?"

Marvin's voice came from behind me. Startled, I turned to see my friend, dressed in denim coveralls today. He carried a large Styrofoam cup in each hand and I watched the steam rising from them. He grinned when he saw my look of surprise.

"You didn't think I would forget the coffee, did you? Old Frank, here, he had a pot already, compliments of the county, so I just got two cups. But I got the thermos in the pickup."

"Have you gone out of your skull, Marvin?" I asked. I felt a frown spreading across my forehead. "Hasn't there been enough tragedy at that place? We're just raising the odds by going back."

"We got to go," Frank said, his voice soft.

For a second, I remembered the masculine voice coming through Moonshadow's lips. I shivered. I looked at Marvin and his eyes held empathy. It was then that I realized neither of them wanted to go, either.

* * *

Our destiny was not to go to the mine at that time, however. Marvin had received a call from the state geological department informing him that two officials should be arriving at Bethel Bluff shortly; he was to show them reports of the tragedy at the Violet Fern. Then he was to escort them to a couple of other mines in the same vicinity. Frank seemed to lose some of his enthusiasm with this disclosure and I told Marvin that Frank and I would wait for him at Gordon's Glen.

"This may take all day, Jackson," the sheriff had said. "These geologists most likely want to establish a connection between the instability at the Violet Fern and the lay of the land at Davis Morgan's mine. We'll have to run down Davis and talk with him. You and Frank go on and find Kyanith."

Frank had been standing to the right side of the doorway and, after Marvin's speculation, he had turned and limped out onto the sidewalk. I looked back at Marvin and then followed my brother.

"I see that Moonshadow is still in town," Frank said over his shoulder. He pointed toward a faded orange Volkswagen bus parked next to my brown Galaxy. I remembered the incident last night at the Lamplighter. Although I was hesitant to risk another encounter with the woman, she *had* cleared my brother and ensured his freedom. And, in the bright light of day, I could almost believe that the events of last night had never happened. *Any* of them.

"Mr. Cody?" The female voice sounded breathless and both Frank and I turned to stare at the tall, slender blonde running across the courthouse green. She wore a navy skirt and vest and a long-sleeved white blouse.

"She works at the bank," Frank said. "You must be the Mr. Cody that she's looking for."

"Are you Jackson Cody?" she asked, stopping directly in front of me. I watched her chest rise and fall under the even knit of her polyester vest.

"I am," I said. "Is there something I can do for you?"

"Yes," she said, taking another deep breath. "I tried to reach you at the motel, but you had already left..."

"And?"

"Your money is here."

"Money?"

"It was wired in from California. From a Mr. Coe Wentworth."

I had already forgotten about the advance promised me for the story. My agent, however, had suffered no such mental lapse. Not having heard from me, he had sent the money to the only bank in the county. Steve Benson's bank. I hesitated.

"You go on, Jackson," Frank said. "I'll find Moonshadow and she can take me to the farm."

I looked at him and nodded absentmindedly. I still had a little cash. Did I need that money badly enough to go and ask for it from Steve Benson? I felt a tug at the elbow of my shirt. Annoyed, I turned sharply and stared angrily at the girl. Vibrant blue eyes, fringed with black, stared curiously back at me. Her porcelain cheeks pinked.

"I'm sorry," she said, dropping her hand to her side. "It's just that this is my break and Mr. Benson docks our paycheck if we take too much time off for break."

"Sure," I said. "My fault. I wasn't thinking. Lead the way."

"I don't think that Mr. Benson intended to tell you," she said when we paused at the street crossing, waiting for a couple of pickups to pass.

"Why do you say *that*?" I asked, grabbing her arm and twisting her around to face me. "Didn't he send you to find me?"

She looked down at my hand circling her upper arm. I pulled it away.

"I don't want to say any more," She told me, looking down, avoiding contact with my eyes. "I have a little girl and this is about the most decent job I can get in Bethel Bluff."

Of course, I thought, following her across the street toward the double doors of a large cream-colored brick building. She had already told me that she was using her break time; she wasn't on bank business. Obviously, Steve Benson was not in his office this morning. My breath, shallow only a moment earlier, deepened, and I followed the girl through the glass doors and into the air-conditioned lobby. A familiar face, now shadowed with gray instead of brown, lighted with recognition and I walked toward Hallie Dumont's teller cage.

"Jackson Cody!" she cried, reaching over the counter and grasping my outstretched hand. "However have you been? What has kept you away so long?"

I relished the feel of Hallie's cool, soft hand in mine. As a teenager, Hallie Addington had worked for Mama Kate, cooking meals and cleaning house during canning season. She had entertained the three of us children on the nights when Mama Kate and Papa Gordon had monitored the vats where the jelly simmered.

"I don't know," I stuttered, lost in the warm depths of her brown eyes. "I hadn't intended to stay away this long."

"I understand," she said, letting my hand go. She flipped through a stack of forms and pulled one out. "Here you go. Fill this out and I'll get your money. It came in two days ago and we were beginning to think you didn't need it."

"I can use it," I told her, picking up a black ballpoint pen from the counter. "How is Curtis? I didn't see him when I came back for Mama Kate's funeral."

Out of the corner of my eye, I watched her busy hands slow and squeeze the cards she had been sorting. Then she tapped the papers on the counter and pulled a thick red rubber band around the stack.

"Curtis died six years ago," she said, her voice tremulous. "The signals weren't working at Deke's Crossing and one of the pulpwood trains hit his car. He was in the hospital for six weeks and, when he came out, he was in a wheelchair."

"God, Hallie. I'm sorry. I didn't know."

Moisture tipped the lashes of her brown eyes and she forced a smile to her lips. I watched helplessly, not knowing what to say, remembering the big, strapping, good-humoured baseball player who had captured her heart and taken her away from Gordon's Glen. Remembering Curtis Dumont.

"He was helpless," she whispered. "Like a baby. I had to feed him, bathe him, see to his personal needs. I didn't mind; I was glad I could do it. But, his mind still belonged to a forty-eight year old and he couldn't stand being helpless. I came home one afternoon and found him on the screened-in porch, his twelve gauge shotgun on the floor beside his wheelchair and pieces of his head sticking to the walls and ceiling of the house."

"I'm sorry," I whispered, reaching for her hand.

56

"I had the screen torn off, Jackson. I kept finding pieces of bone wedged in the mesh."

I reached across the counter and pulled the upper part of her body to my chest, holding her until I felt her quivering subside. Then I relaxed my hold and watched her straighten her navy blue vest and pat her hair. Determination forced a pleasant smile to her face.

"I'm sorry, hon," she said. "You've had your problems, too, with Liz and this mess that's happened. Here, let me have the card and I'll get your cash."

I watched her as she talked with another blue-uniformed lady in a glassed-in enclosure toward the rear of the bank. They both looked at me and smiled. The red-headed one waved a shy hand. I raised my own in salutation. Something about her was familiar, but I couldn't quite place her.

"Here you go," Hallie said, walking back and handing me a bulging white envelope. "Don't spend it all in one place."

I smiled back at her, feeling the reassuring thickness of the envelope. I remembered the same caution from my childhood whenever I got my allowance.

"I always spent it all in the same place, Hallie. Remember? You would bring the three of us to town and I'd go straight to the bookrack at the drugstore."

"All three of you were predictable," she agreed. "Liz bought art supplies and Frank bought cap pistols or rubber swords."

I grinned. It had been years since I had thought of the hours I'd spent in that building. I could almost smell the sawdust and oil smell of the hardwood floor, the paper and ink scent of a new book.

"Hallie, who's the redhead? The one you were talking to?"

"That's Susan. Surely you remember her. Susan and Liz were the same age. The best of friends."

"Susan *who*?"

"Susan Benson. Steve's sister."

How could I have failed to recognize Susan Benson, I chastised myself as I left the bank and walked back toward the jail. Susan Benson had provided the white that was a direct contrast for her brother's black. That was too many years ago, I thought, shaking my head. Too much water had gone under the bridge.

By the time I reached the Ford Galaxy, Moonshadow's orange bus was gone. Looking around, I couldn't see Frank and supposed, just as he promised, that he had talked her into taking him to the farm. I opened the door on the driver's side and felt hot air rush out to meet me. Praying that the air-conditioner still worked, I slid onto the hot seat and tucked the envelope in the compartment between the two bucket seats. The keys still rested in the ignition where I had left them. I turned the key and the engine rumbled to life. I would pick up Frank and then we would go to the mine. Despite my dread at the prospect, I wanted this entire episode over, forgotten, out of the picture.

The engine provided background accompaniment for still another sound and I looked up and through the windshield to see Marvin rushing toward me, his mouth moving. I shut off the engine and leaned out the window.

"Change your mind?" I asked. "Or did the state department of geology decide they could make do without you?"

"Neither," he said, his mouth stern. "That trip is still on. I have a message for you."

"Oh?"

"Now, don't get all bent out of shape when I tell you. Susan Benson just called me from the bank and asked me if I could persuade you to meet her at the park in fifteen minutes."

"Susan Benson? The park?"

"Yeah, Susan. In case you can't remember her, Susan is the total opposite to Steve. She's one of the sweetest human beings I've ever known."

"Okay, Marvin. I don't remember her very well." I hesitated at the lie. "But, I'll take your word for it. What does she want to talk about?"

"She didn't tell me and it wasn't my business to ask. Do you remember how to get to the park?"

Chapter Eight

Beartrack Mountain, accessible only by an unimproved county road and six miles from downtown Bethel Bluff, rose steeply out of a lush meadow a thousand feet below the summit. The park itself was tucked into one of the hollows created by a million or so years of rainfall tumulting down the rugged sides of the mountain. I eased the Galaxy into a graveled parking area beside the weathered pavilion, next to a fairly new, economy sized Chevrolet.

Unfolding my body, I climbed out of the hot car, grateful for the light breeze that ruffled the leafy shade around me. Down past the pavilion, just under the hill, I saw the glint of sunlight on water. Susan Benson must be down by the lake. I found the brown sign designating the hiking path and wove my way through the underbrush, emerging only moments later at the large pond an oldtimer had named Serenity Lake.

She sat on a wooden bench, her back to me, gazing out over the waters. Despite the shapeless blue knit uniform, I could detect the ample female curves of her body. Back stiff, legs crossed at the ankles, fingers tight on the planks on either side of her body, she seemed poised for flight, as skittish as one of the water birds at the lake's edge.

"Susan?"

She flinched and then turned her head to watch me scramble down the steep path toward her. Her defensive posture had prepared me for a look of guilt, apology, or even fear. But her face portrayed peace, resignation.

"I'm glad you came, Jackson," she said, standing up and offering me a slender hand. "I didn't know if you would."

I grasped her hand for a moment before letting go. The moisture on her palm belied her calm demeanor.

"You enlisted the right person to convince me," I said. "Marvin has

59

always been able to influence me."

"I was hoping that it was still that way," she said. "Jackson, I need your help."

"*My* help?" I asked. "What could I possibly do for *you*?" I looked at the expensive diamond and emerald ring on her right hand, the cut of her reptile shoes. "I would think that your brother could do more for you than I could."

She closed her eyes, just an infinite moment longer than a blink. I watched the muscles of her throat move when she swallowed. When she opened her eyes, I sensed, rather than saw, the desperation hidden behind them.

"I want you to help me save Kyanith."

"Kyanith?" I gasped. "I'm sorry if I seem a bit dense, but why are you concerned about Kyanith's welfare?"

A frown furrowed her forehead and her eyes searched mine. Then she turned her face back toward the lake.

"There's a picnic table over there," she said, pointing to a spot about a third of the way around the lake. "Not too many people know about it. I don't think we'll be disturbed."

"Wait, Susan," I protested. "I don't have very much time. There's a lot I need to do. The mine. Frank. Kyanith..."

"If you're really concerned," she said, striding down to the lake's edge. "Then you'll listen to me."

"Okay," I said, detesting the hesitation in my voice. "I'll listen."

"Thanks, Jackson," she said, smiling broadly. She impulsively grabbed my hand. "Right over there. Behind those big rocks."

"First of all," Susan said, once we were seated at the wooden picnic table, she on one side and I on the other, "let me assure you that, at the moment, Kyanith is fine and in no immediate danger."

"You've talked to her?"

"We've communicated."

I didn't want to hear that. I wanted Susan to be specific, to tell me that she had s*een* Kyanith, had *talked* to her on the telephone. But, indifferent to my desires, Susan continued.

"My brother is obsessed with hatred and envy," she said. "He wants to eliminate the Anderson family from the face of the earth. He's prepared to use any means necessary to accomplish that end."

"I think I'm beginning to realize that."

"But, you don't know the extremes to which Steve will go. Or, how many people he will destroy who are in his way."

"Susan, are you telling me that Steve was responsible for Liz's and Jace Wright's deaths?"

"No," she said, shaking her head. "Not directly, at least."

"Susan, I think you'd better start at the beginning."

Her shoulders rose and fell as she breathed deeply. Her eyes shone with unshed tears. With an unsteady hand, she brushed back a lock of sandy-red hair that had fallen across her forehead.

"I suppose it started when Gordon bought a thousand acres of rocky, hilly, nonproductive land from my grandfather, Hiram."

"I didn't know that. Gordon's Glen belonged to the Benson's?"

"It wasn't Gordon's Glen, then. It was a no-good tax burden. The crops that Grandfather knew how to farm wouldn't grow on that property and he hadn't paid taxes on it for years. Gordon Anderson paid him more than fair market value for that type of acreage."

"I don't understand, then, why there was a problem, any reason for resentment."

Susan smiled, a tight, straight smile that thinned her lips. Her green eyes remained neutral.

"There wasn't, at first," she said. "Grandfather Benson went to his grave a happy man, proud of his skill at making the deal. It was Grandmother who was responsible for the bitterness."

"Your *grandmother*?"

Susan nodded. She clasped her hands together tightly on the surface of the table.

"My grandmother didn't die until I was twelve, so I heard the story hundreds, even thousands of times. It was always the same version, almost identical words, no variations. As if it were a fable or a poem she had memorized. She had practiced on Daddy, but she perfected every nuance with Steve. It's taken me a lot of my own life to sort out the truth from the fiction.

"Gordon Anderson came to Bethel Bluff with more money than most people around here had ever seen. As I said before, he paid Grandfather more money than that land was worth. I'm assuming that my grandmother was pleased about the sale until Gordon's orchards and vineyards began producing. Then, somehow or another, her thinking became twisted, almost paranoid.

"I believe now that Grandmother saw the cash dwindling that Gordon had given Grandfather. At the same time, the poor, barren land that Grandfather had sold to Gordon sprang to life, green and rich with fruit. Gordon built a large house with several outbuildings and he began courting the girl that Grandmother had chosen for her own son, Alvin."

"Mama Kate?" I asked, startled.

Susan laughed then, a genuine display of mirth. Then she calmed and reached across the table to pat my hand.

"Jackson, you've spent too much of your life with your nose stuck in a book. You've missed reality. Not Mama Kate."

"I don't understand."

"Gordon Anderson fell head over heels in love with Sarah Tillery."

"My *mother*?"

"Yes. It was assumed that Gordon and Sarah would be married."

"I never knew."

"It was common knowledge, Jackson."

"God," I said, stifling a silly grin. "Your father, my father, and Papa Gordon, all in love with my mother. What about your father? How did he take it? When did my dad come into the picture?"

"My father was a placid, easily contented man. Despite Grandmother's propaganda, he married my mother three months after being jilted by Sarah and I don't think he ever regretted a minute of their marriage. Grandmother, of course, never liked my mother and made life miserable for her, constantly reminding her that she was not good enough for Daddy.

"As for Elmer Cody, your father. From what I gather, he was a dashing, romantic, diamond-in-the-rough sort. Some women are irresistibly attracted to these fun-loving, carefree, irresponsible men and feel the need to take care of them. Apparently, your mother felt that Elmer needed her and that Gordon didn't."

"She loved Papa Gordon until she died," I said, amazed at the words coming out of my mouth. I remembered the conversation outside the bedroom window the night my father died. "I just assumed that they loved each other as brother and sister."

"Now you know."

"Yeah. But, getting back to your story, your grandmother attempted to turn your father against Papa Gordon, but failed in her efforts."

"Daddy just plowed along, using Grandfather's money to buy the gas station out at the junction. He and my mother worked fourteen and sixteen hours a day until they had enough money to double the size of the building and open a grocery store and, then, a couple of years later, the gift shop.

"In the meantime," she continued. "Grandmother practically raised

Steve and me. I was lucky; she didn't like me. But she must have seen a lot of herself in Steve. She told him biased versions of the land acquisition, of Gordon's stealing Alvin's promised bride. By the time Steve was eight years old, he was convinced that Gordon's Glen was rightfully his. I think he actually hated Daddy because Daddy wouldn't fight for it."

"That *is* rough," I said, remembering the loving atmosphere I'd known as a child. "Your childhood must have been terribly lonesome. Your mother and father had each other. Your grandmother and Steve had each other..."

"If I had been given the choice, that would have been the decision I would have made for myself," Susan said, smiling. Her eyes looked into the distance. "Personality-wise, I'm a loner. Even as a tot, I spent hours inside my head, thinking and dreaming. By the time I felt the need for companionship, I was in school and Liz was there."

"You two were almost inseparable."

"Much to Grandmother's chagrin and displeasure," Susan admitted. "There were many times that she tried to poison our relationship, but failed. The friendship we had together was too strong for a mortal to destroy."

I debated asking her to explain what she meant. Was she implying that the relationship had ended? That she and Liz had been torn apart by something supernatural?

"Grandmother taught Steve to hate the Anderson family and that included you and Frank, especially since you two were Sarah Tillery's children. She convinced Steve that you boys thought you were better than he was. She distorted every imagined slight that Steve told her about. On your tenth birthday, when Steve was six, Mrs. Anderson had a party for you and Frank. I never questioned the reason, but Steve was the only boy at the elementary school who didn't get an invitation."

"But he did," I protested. "I gave it to him myself. I remember vividly. I handed it to him on the playground."

Susan shrugged her shoulders. Again, she smiled the thin smile.

"Already, even at that age, he was lying to please Grandmother. He thought she was some sort of saint. I think the only time my brother ever felt pain or grief was when he was fourteen and Grandmother died. He didn't even close the bank for Daddy's funeral last year."

"So you feel that the only thing he wants now is to own Gordon's Glen? And Kyanith is in the way? But, he holds the mortgage. Liz signed the farm over to him as collateral for that loan!"

63

"The loan is paid off, Jackson. It was paid off last week, right before Liz was killed."

"No! Who did *that*?"

Susan looked down at the table, at her clenched hands. Her mouth twitched.

"It couldn't have been Frank," I speculated. "Marvin doesn't have that kind of money, nor does Kyanith. Moonshadow! She had enough money. But, *why*?"

Susan's white face ashed to a pale gray. The freckles across the bridge of her nose stood out boldly.

"It was a mistake, Jackson," she stumbled. "I thought it would change the direction that things were going. I was sure that it would make Steve stop and reconsider the results of his actions..."

"*You*!" I gasped. "*You* paid off the loan?"

"I had the money, Jackson. It seemed to me that if there were no loan, Liz and Frank would halt the mad idea of mining the Violet Fern. Kyanith's heritage would be assured, and Steve's plans would be thwarted. I thought that it would jolt him back to a semblance of sanity."

"But, Susan," I said, reaching over to take her cold hands in mine. "They couldn't have known about your Samatarian deed. I know that Frank didn't! He's sure that the loan is still outstanding. I'm positive that Liz would have cancelled any work at the mine if..."

"She knew, Jackson. I told her."

"And she went back to the mine, anyway? Are you sure that she *understood* you?"

Susan nodded. Her lips trembled and I looked away from her, across the lake and toward the mountain. Why would Liz have done such a thing?

Chapter Nine

"Good God, Susan! She was crazy! Why didn't somebody do something about her?"

"Have her committed?"

"I suppose so."

"It would have been difficult to obtain a court order to send her to the state hospital for psychiatric observation. And I'm sure it would have been almost impossible to prove any emotional abnormality. Liz was as sane as you or me. She just had periods when parts of her didn't seem to be there."

"Marvin said she was empty. I believe he used the expression 'hollowed-out.' Now you tell me that parts of her were missing. What the hell am I supposed to think?"

"When did you last see Liz?"

"The week of Mama Kate's funeral," I snapped. Although Susan's question was asked in a neutral tone, I found myself responding defensively. "My work in California kept me away. If I'd had any idea how bad things were..."

"What would you have done differently?"

"Susan, you're forcing me to dig more deeply into myself than I want. I don't suppose I would have behaved any differerently. I was pretty wrapped up in myself and what was happening to me. I didn't do a lot of thinking about my family here in Bethel Bluff. When I did, I always thought of them as strong, healthy, and fit. The way they were when I was a kid. I've got to know, though, what happened to Liz."

Susan pulled herself to her feet and turned toward the lake. She took a few steps toward the water and then halted, hugging her arms to her chest. When she turned back to me, tears made twin streams down her cheeks.

"Walk with me, Jackson. There's a trail all the way around the lake, now. The Youth Corps cleared it last summer."

I nodded and stood up, feeling a weakness behind my knees. The breeze that had been so welcome a short time earlier now caused a chill to ripple down my back. Susan had already begun walking the path and I hurried after her.

"You mentioned it earlier," she said, over her shoulder. "Liz and I were together constantly all the way through school. As you remember, we attended the same college and even pledged the same sorority. Until the last semester of our senior year, we dated only guys who knew each other so that we could double-date and go to the same places."

"What happened at that time?"

"Her friendship with Jason Cartwright grew into a more serious relationship and she began spending more time alone with him. During that semester, I was assigned to a school several miles away to do my student teaching. Two other girls and I rented an apartment and I returned to the campus only on weekends."

"So Liz started changing when she became romantically involved with Cartwright?"

We were halfway around the lake now and Susan halted so abruptly that I almost bumped into her, Keystone Cops style. She turned to face me.

"No!" she cried. "It's such a difficult thing to explain. I've never even tried to tell anyone before. I felt that I owed it to Liz to remain silent."

"Look, Susan," I said, taking her arm and leading her off the path, toward the woods. "Sit down here on this log with me and just take your time."

She didn't protest, but I felt her body stiffen as I eased her to a sitting position on the trunk of the fallen tree. I sat down beside her and placed my right arm around her shoulders.

"For as long as I can remember," Susan began. "Liz had this adorable little habit of kidding away praise given to her. In college, she received several awards for her artwork, especially her sculptures. If, at any time, she was required to give an acceptance speech, she always ended it with, 'I owe it all to Andy.'"

"Andy? Frank mentioned an Andy. He seemed to think that Andy was a close friend from college."

"No, I'll explain later. Just let me continue with this thought."

"Of course," I agreed.

"Any time that Liz was complimented for her creative work or

66

talent, she gave Andy credit. On the other hand, if anyone noticed or commented on her buoyant personality, her loving nature, or her ability to bring out the best in people, she told them that her personality was due to Betsy's influence."

"Betsy! That's the other name that Frank mentioned. Oops, sorry."

"Now, if her sense of duty or responsibility was admired, or her ability to remain calm in a crisis, she accepted the praise as her own. That part of her was Liz."

Susan paused for a moment as if she hoped I would fully grasp the entire situation and she wouldn't have to explain any more. But I wouldn't let her off that easily.

"Go on, Susan. So far, I follow you."

"When I returned to campus after my student teaching, Liz told me that she and Jason planned to marry immediately after graduation in two months. I knew that Jason had already signed with a professional football team on the east coast and I was concerned that Liz would be forced to sublimate or change her own goals and desires."

"How's that, Susan? Which goals and desires?"

"For as long as I can remember, Liz had planned for a career. She wanted to actively pursue her art and, if she had the time, teach art classes. She had drawn a picture of her New York studio so clearly with words that she had only to mention it and I saw every chair, every table, every picture on the wall."

"And this would have been impossible if she had married Jason?"

"Yes," Susan said, nodding. She shifted her position on the log, crossing her left leg over her right. "I confronted her with the idea, taking the chance that the conversation might seriously damage our friendship."

"How did she react?"

"She was Liz. How else can I explain it? She threw her arms around me, laughing and crying at the same time, and told me how much she loved me for my concern, but that everything would work out fine. She would sinply postpone her career for a few years. In the meantime, she said, she would be the charming, loving, supportive wife. She would be Betsy."

"She said that? She said that she would be *Betsy*?"

"Jackson, don't you see? Liz called her creative aspect Andy. The nurturing part of herself she named Betsy, and her responsible self retained the label Liz."

"Elizabeth Anderson," I said, rolling the syllables over my tongue.

"Each of the names was part of the greater name."

"And each of the selves," Susan whispered. "Was a part of the greater self."

"We're all composed of a number of personality traits," I defended. "We would be flat creatures if we lived only one of our aspects..."

I stopped, silenced by Susan's grim stare. Her green eyes challenged me to complete my speculation, but I couldn't continue.

"Liz decided to temporarily suppress the Andy part of her personality," Susan said. "And she seemed to be handling it well. A couple of weeks after this decision, she brought Jason to Bethel Bluff to meet her parents. It was her first trip home in weeks and she was horrified to find that Mama Kate had shriveled away to almost nothing. When Liz managed to find the time alone and talk with her mother, Mama Kate admitted that she was dying, but she made Liz promise to finish school and marry Jason, to go on with her life, regardless of what happened."

"The loving compassionate part," I speculated, "the Betsy part, promised her mother she would obey her wishes."

"Liz was heartbroken when she returned to college after that trip," Susan continued. "She wanted to be at Bethel Bluff with her parents, but she had given her mother her word. And then, almost immediately, Mrs. Anderson died."

I reached down and picked up a decaying oak twig from the ground. I rolled it between my palms for a few seconds, watching the loose, dry bark peel away and float to the ground.

"As you remember, the funeral was scheduled for the middle of the week," Susan said.

"Wednesday, as I recall."

"Yes. Liz absolutely forbade either Jason or me to come with her, as it was test week and missing that time might hinder our chances for graduation. I could have cared less because, to me, being with Liz was much more important than graduating from college."

"I understand," I said, dropping the mutilated twig to the ground.

"But she convinced me, finally, that she needed to be alone. And I respected her wishes. I'm sure that Jason felt the same."

"Sure."

"Jason loved Liz, don't ever question that. I'm not sure I've ever seen that amount of love lavished on anyone since."

"Then, why didn't he stand by her side, marry her, come back here and help her?"

"I'll get to that part of the story, Jackson. Just be patient."

I sighed, a deep breath that came out almost as a snort. "Liz didn't return to campus until Sunday night..."

"Wait," I exclaimed. "That couldn't be. I was here and I remember that Liz left right after the funeral. I stayed on a couple of days at the house; I should know!"

"I didn't say that Liz stayed here at Gordon's Glen. I didn't even say that she stayed at Bethel Bluff. I'm just giving you an idea of the time passage before Jason and I saw her."

"*Where* was she?" I demanded angrily. "I wanted to see her and talk, but she left too soon."

"I'm not sure," Susan said. "I think she might have been at the old hunting cabin."

"Up by the Violet Fern?"

Susan nodded.

"She had done a lot of thinking," she continued. "And planning. The promise she had made her mother was weighing heavily on her. She told me that she and her mother had spent the last three days discussing that promise."

"And you believed her? Mama Kate was *dead*!"

"Grief has a tendency to open you to other levels of communication, Jackson. I believe that there's an existence after death. Call it Heaven, Nirvana, whatever you want. If the desire is there, two beings can communicate."

"That's a crock! You're as crazy as she was!"

"Perhaps," Susan said calmly. "However, I'm relating the story, as you requested."

"I'm sorry."

"It seems that the outcome of the discussion was that Liz was to return to college and Mrs. Anderson would send her some sort of sign to help her make the decision."

"Gordon's stroke," I interjected.

"I know that you think this could be a script for a science fiction movie, Jackson. But, that was the way that it happened. She was with Jason when the word came. Daddy called me and I took the bus over to Jason's dorm. They were sitting out back, in some lounge chairs, just watching the sunset. When I told Liz, Jason grabbed her hand, as if to hold her there. I could almost see the electric current passing through their hands, from his body to hers. She squeezed his fingers and then she stood up, pale and trembling. 'This is it, Jason,' she said. 'It's what I have to do. From this point on, it's *my* responsibility.' He looked at her, pain making his eyes enormous and his face rigid. Then we walked away and Liz didn't look back."

"He just let her go?"

"I would think that the highest form of love is to respect another's wishes. To let that person have the freedom to do what he or she feels that he or she has to do."

"Even if *he* or *she* is crazy?"

"That is your interpretation, Jackson," she said stiffly, "and not necessarily an accurate diagnosis."

"I think you're all crazy," I said, standing up and brushing bark off of my pants. "The whole damned bunch here at Bethel Bluff has gone off their collective gourds!"

"Then you probably aren't interested in the rest of the crazy story."

* * *

I should have walked away at that moment, but I sensed a challenge in Susan's words. That, coupled with my deepening curiousity, compelled me to sit back down on the log beside her.

"If I don't hear it from you," I said, resigned, "I'll have to find out from someone else."

"I don't know if there is anyone left who could tell you," she said. "Although Marvin Garland could probably give you the most unprejudiced version of the homecoming and ensuing years."

"I'll listen. And I'll try to avoid making judgements."

"Liz came back to Bethel Bluff at the end of April," Susan began.

"And Jason?"

"In spite of his grief, he graduated and went to New York to play football. He and I agreed to keep in touch and I promised to notify him as soon as Liz asked for him. If necessary, he was prepared to spend the rest of his life on the farm here at Bethel Bluff."

"Being a Hollywood actor is a far cry from being an Arkansas farmer."

"Don't be facetious, Jackson. Jason would have done anything to be with Liz if she wanted him."

"What about Kyanith? Did he ever stop to think that s*he* might need him?"

"He didn't know about Kyanith."

"He didn't *know*?"

"Liz didn't want him to know. She said she would tell Kyanith when the time was right."

"And Liz, naturally, would decide the right time."

Susan leaped to her feet and moved stiffly toward a halfgrown pine at the edge of the clearing. She leaned against the tree, resting her face against the brownish-gray bark. I watched her shoulders heave.

"You self-righteous, pompous, arrogant hypocrite! Don't blame us. We did everything we could do. There was never anything here that kept *you* from returning!"

She had turned to face me during her tirade and I watched her face redden as tears trickled down her cheeks. White patches developed around her mouth and her nose.

"How can you pretend such outrage at *our* actions," she said between clenched teeth. "When you never even bothered to call! At least we *tried*!"

"Hey, Susan," I said, walking toward her. "I didn't intend to criticize you. I'm sure you did the best you..."

"Don't patronize me," she snapped. "And don't come any closer! I don't want you to touch me again. Get away from me!"

She stepped back from me as I reached for her arm. Snagging on an ancient tree root, her high heeled navy pump turned and she lost her balance, slipping to her knees. I caught her upper arms before she could fall on the sharp rocks.

"Turn me loose," she gritted, pulling against my grasp and struggling to regain her balance.

"Quit pulling away from me," I said. "I'm not going to hurt you. You're the last person in the world I'd want to hurt."

"You said that before," she whimpered, slapping at my hands. "Damn you, Jackson Cody. Where do you get off, coming back here after all those years with your holier-than-thou attitude, telling me what I've done wrong? Where were you when I needed you?"

I loosened my grip on her arms and she pulled loose, stepping away from me. Her green eyes blazed accusation.

"*You* needed me?" I laughed. "You've never needed anybody, Susan Benson. I've never known a more self-sufficient woman, unless it was Liz."

A low rumble in the distance shook the earth and Susan flinched, glancing over her shoulder. her face blanched.

"Did you hear that?" she gasped. "Did you *feel* it?"

"Yeah," I said. I looked up at the blue sky, searching for the telltale cumulonimbus cloud, a sure sign of an approaching thunderstorm.

"You needn't bother looking for clouds," Susan said. "It wasn't thunder."

"Well, then. What *was* it?"

"The mine," she said, her voice low. "It's the Violet Fern."

"Susan..."

"You don't know, Jackson. You don't understand."

"Try me."

"You'll only ridicule me."

"Susan, I promise I won't. I'll do my best to understand. Let me help"

She looked at me, her eyes steady. With a graceful movement of her slender neck, she tossed her red hair back from her face. She held out her right hand to me, a silent apology.

"Then take me to the mine, Jackson. Kyanith is there."

Chapter Ten

"Hey, wait a second," I yelled. "I need to rest."

"We don't have time," Susan yelled back at me. Through the late afternoon light, I could see her slender figure about a hundred feet ahead of me, relentlessly pushing up the steep trail. "It's almost dark and I'm not sure I can find the cabin at night."

"You're sure that Kyanith is at the cabin?"

"Positive."

"Okay," I yelled. "Pick up your feet, girl, and lead the way."

Determined to make the best of a bad situation, to save Susan and Kyanith, even if I'd failed when the others had needed me, I had agreed to go with Susan to the cabin. We had stopped by her house in order for her to change into blue jeans and walking shoes. Then we had driven out to her mother's house to borrow her father's old jeep.

I was glad now that I hadn't protested when Susan had dug through a closet and found an old pair of men's hiking boots. I was glad I had resisted the impulse to ask if they were Steve's, when Susan had apologized, saying that they had belonged to her ex-husband. I was even happier when they had fit; this last leg of the trip would have torn my canvas shoes to shreds.

"Are you sure we're on the right road?" I yelled.

Susan stopped and turned back to face me. She rested her right hand on her hip and waited.

"I admit you expertise," I placated, faking a courtly bow. "If I remember correctly, I was up here the last time when I was fifteen. Papa Gordon, Frank, and I spent the night at the cabin after we had wandered all over the mountain pretending to track deer."

"*You* were pretending," Susan giggled. "Frank was very serious, I'm sure. He probably couldn't wait to test one of his new rifles."

Susan's laugh warmed me. For a moment, I could pretend that we

73

were simply old friends who had been reunited after several years' absence. For a few precious seconds, I could forget our reason for being here, the tragedy that had brought us together. But Susan reminded me.

"Did you tell Martha to give Marvin the message tonight?"

"I'm not sure that I was that specific," I said, remembering my rush into Marvin's office earlier that afternoon. He had still been out with the geologists, but his clerk had promised to tell him that Susan and I were going to the mine.

"That's not so good," Susan said, her shoulders dropping. "He may not be able to get out here until mid-morning."

"I don't know what he could do before that."

"Neither do I," Susan admitted. "But his presence would surely be a comfort."

"I agree," I said, reaching for her hand. "But we'll make it, Superwoman. Lead the way."

She giggled again and slipped her left arm around my waist. I found myself wondering how I had let Chris and the bright lights of Hollywood blind me to my first love. I put my arm around Susan's shoulders, feeling her warm flesh underneath the thin chambray shirt. She squeezed my waist and matched her step to mine.

"Your ex-husband," I began, picking my way over a series of ruts. "What was he like?"

"Wes? He was a good person. Warm. Compassionate."

"Why did you divorce him?"

She sighed. I sensed, rather than felt, her pull away.

"I'm sorry Susan. Don't answer that. It's none of my business."

"It doesn't really matter anymore, Jackson. At one time, it grieved me that I had failed so miserably. Then I learned to accept the fact that, although we had both grown while being married, we had each grown in different directions. It didn't come to an abrupt end; the marriage just faded. There was never any hostility, just disillusionment."

"I wish I could say the same."

"I know," Susan said. "I followed all the Hollywood scandal sheets. Frankly, I could never understand what you saw in Chris Vining."

"As another woman, you wouldn't," I said, stepping to the left to avoid a deep hole. "She was physically attractive…"

"Definitely," Susan said, swerving to the right to miss the same hole.

"We knew a lot of the same people," I continued. "And she played on my ego. She flattered me and I fell for it."

74

The gathering darkness didn't quite hid the wide smile on Susan's lips. I smiled back. The I felt the blood in my body turn to ice. Susan sensed my stiffness.

"What's wrong?" she asked, turning to look the direction I'd been facing. Then the life left her voice. "Oh, my God. Kyanith..."

"What is it?" I demanded. "Is the cabin on fire?"

"No. The cabin is on the side of the hill, over to our left. The mine is straight ahead. That's where the light is coming from."

"Have you ever seen anything like it?" I asked, remembering Marvin's tale of the eerie blue light hanging over the tunnel at the Violet Fern.

"I've heard about it," Susan said, drawing closer to me. "But I've never seen it. It's weird. What do you think causes it? Some sort of gas?"

"I hope so," I said. "I hope to God that it's caused by gases."

Directly ahead of us, only a few hundred yards away, the unearthly blue light shimmered and seemed to grow. Then it decreased in both intensity and volume. The pine trees near the mine clearing, silhouetted by the light, leaned back and forth. I felt as if the light were alive, some sort of protoplasm, threatening to engulf us.

"It's just a few more steps up here to the fork," Susan said, her voice uneven. "We turn to the left and go down through the draw."

"Let's go," I said, pulling her along. "The sooner we get away from that creepy light, the better I'll like it."

We were almost to the creek before I felt the weight lift from my shoulders. I turned to look behind me. The blue light had disappeared.

"It's gone, Susan," I said. "We can stop for a few minutes."

"Good. I need to get the flashlight from my backpack. It's going to be rough enough crossing that creek, even with a light."

Chapter Eleven

Crossing the small stream proved no easy task. In the darkness, the slippery creek rocks formed, at best, a precarious bridge across the swiftly moving waters. At one point, about two thirds of the way across, my right foot slipped and I stumbled into the chill of the spring-fed waters, gasping hoarsely as I fumbled to regain my balance.

"What's wrong?" Susan, ahead of me and almost to the far bank, yelled over her shoulder.

"Nothing," I groaned, feeling for a more stable foothold with my already soaked boot. "I just slipped."

"Well, be careful," she said. "You'll break a leg if you don't watch what you're doing."

"How am I supposed to watch my step? I can't even see my feet!"

"Don't complain," Susan giggled. "I haven't been able to see mine for three months!"

"You can't blame me for that!" I yelled back, slipping into the spirit of her joviality. "It's not my fault."

"The hell it's not," she shouted. "Hurry. We'll stop here at the josta."

"The *what*?"

Then, as if illuminated by some secret light, a small, greenhouse-like building to the right side of the trail glowed into being, silhouetting Susan's body. My breath caught in my throat.

"Susan," I gasped, staring at the bulk of her middle body. "I didn't realize you were pregnant!"

"Oh, Campbell," she moaned, plucking at the sleeve of my jacket and pulling me to a bench along the inner wall of the tiny building. "Please don't start with that again."

"Start with what?" I demanded. "What are you talking about? You weren't pregnant this afternoon. What, in God's name, is a josta? And, why are you calling me Campbell?"

Beside me, on the metallic-feeling bench, Susan bent her neck and dropped her face into her cupped hands. Her shoulders shook.

"It's been so long," she sobbed, her voice muffled. "I thought it was over. I was sure that it wouldn't happen again."

"Tell me Susan," I said, more gently this time. I curved my right arm around her heaving shoulders. "I apologize for upsetting you. Just tell me what is happening. I don't understand."

She raised her head and looked at me, red-rimmed eyes staring out from her tear-streaked face. I watched her throat muscles swell as she swallowed.

"Please stay calm," she whispered. "I'll call Katie. She'll help."

I watched her touch one of the dull stones on the thick silver wristband she wore. It glowed brightly for a second and then returned to a neutral color. What the hell, I told myself. It's a dream and, since I'm alert enough to realize the phenomena, I'll play along.

"Tell me about Katie," I began pleasantly. Susan stiffened and the green eyes that stared at me were wide and full of fear. I gently squeezed her shoulders and felt her pull away. Then she looked over my head and relaxed. I turned to see a tall, middle-aged Indian woman standing in the doorway. Katie, I surmised, silently awed by the manner in which dreams worked. All one had to do was to mention a person and he or she is there, with no time passage observed. I watched her walk toward me and realized, with shock, why she was so familiar. My dream Katie was Mama Kate!

"How long?" she asked Susan as she knelt on the floor beside me and took my left hand in her warm, calloused ones.

"Twenty minutes, at the most," Susan answered. "It must have happened when we crossed the stream. Before that, he was perfectly normal."

Mama Kate nodded and moved her hands to my shoulders, pulling my head toward her. Her dark eyes stared into mine. Without dropping her gaze, she directed another question to Susan.

"What were you talking about?"

"The baby," Susan said. She paused for a moment. "His new novel."

Mama Kate had her hands on each side of my head now, gently rubbing circular motions on my temples. Her eyelids dropped and flickered. Her breathing deepened, then slowed.

"What else?" she gasped hoarsely. "Think Miranda, you discussed something else. This state was triggered by something that happened or was said."

"The old gold mine on the mountain," Susan whispered. "We were discussing the possibility of utilizing the crystals around the old tunnel. He thought they could amplify the generator's energy and we could be practically free of the need for uranium."

"The tunnel?" Mama Kate queried. Her neutral tone belied the start I'd felt her make when the mine had been mentioned. She turned my head back toward her and forced my gaze to hers. I felt myself being drawn into the deep magnetic pools of her liquid brown eyes.

"Are you there, Etal?" she asked, her palms hot on my cheeks. I felt myself being drawn into a whirlpool and I tried to shake it away. I didn't like the feeling of being unable to control this dream.

"No!" I cried. "I'm Jackson. Jackson Cody! I'm tired of this dream and I want to end it!"

"This is a new one," Susan/Miranda whispered to Mama Kate/ Katie. "He's never brought forth this personality."

I felt tiny prickles of something akin to electrical currents pass from Mama Kate's palms to my cheeks and then vibrate through my body. Pictures of Susan, Mama Kate and me flashed across the insides of my closed eyelids. In one picture, Papa Gordon and my mother, Sarah, were with us; in another, Liz and Frank stood to the side. In yet another, Steve Benson and Marvin sat, conversing pleasantly in a musical language I seemed to understand.

"He's slipping away, Miranda."

It was Mama Kate's voice, concerned. I grabbed her hands and pressed them harder against my cheeks.

"Etal! Etal, listen to me! You must find Kyanith and tell her of this. Do you understand me?"

I nodded dumbly. It was hot and the electrical current from Mama Kate/Katie's hands had concentrated into a pressure point in the middle of my forehead. I willed myself to awaken.

"Jackson? Jackson, are you okay?"

It was Susan's voice. I slowly opened my eyes, squinting against the force of bright light shining directly into my face.

"Jackson?"

"Yeah," I answered, turning my eyes away from the light and toward the welcome darkness. The josta was gone and Mama Kate/ Katie along with it. Cold water lapped against my left side and I realized that I lay at the edge of the spring-fed stream.

"God," Susan giggled shakily. "You scared me. I couldn't see myself carrying you all the way back up that hill to the jeep. Here, grab my hand and let's get you out of that water."

I reached for her hand and paused. I needed another answer.

"Susan, are you pregnant?"

"Of course I'm not," she laughed. "Unless you believe in immaculate conception and I'm a chosen vehicle."

"I'm not sure what I believe," I grunted, reaching for her outstretched hand. "I just had the strangest dream."

"Dream? You weren't down for more than a minute. What kind of dream could you have had? Here, watch yourself or you're going to end up back in the creek. There, step on that rock, then that one. Yeah, you're okay. Did you hit your head?"

"I don't think so. But my legs still feel wobbly. Is there some place around here to sit down for a few minutes?"

"Just rocks," Susan said. "But we can find some flat ones."

I followed the conical beam of light projected by the flashlight she carried. Up ahead, on our right, a long ledge of gray rocks appeared.

"Here," she said, pointing the light toward a sandstone shelf about three feet long and a foot deep. I slumped on the primitive sofa and felt the comforting warmth of her body as she eased down beside me. She flicked off the light and the mellow darkness drifted down around us.

"Susan?"

"Yes?"

"Have you ever heard of a josta?"

Almost imperceptibly, I felt her pull away from me. After a moment, she replied.

"I can't say that I have."

I wished for a light. I would have liked to have seen her face. I found myself growing impatient with her ambiguous replies. What did she know about me that she had no intention of telling me? I was struggling for a way to word my next question when she abruptly stood up and switched the flashlight back on.

"We need to get on up to the cabin and get you dried off," she said, turning the light toward the dim footpath. "It can't be too much farther."

The steep climb eliminated further opportunity for questions on my part. Later, I promised myself. Later, I would get some answers from Susan and I would show no mercy. My compassionate days were nearing an end.

"Just a bit farther," Susan said, from a distance several feet up the trail. I squinted my eyes against the intrusive glare of the flashlight as she swung the beam around toward me.

"Go on," I told her. "I'll catch up. Right now, I have to stop and catch my breath."

I leaned against the rough bark of a pine sapling next to the trail's edge, forcing my breath to regulate and my heartbeat to slow. It had been a long time and I hadn't realized how badly I had let my body get out of shape. I watched the bobbing of the light before Susan turned it back down the trail toward me.

"I can see the cabin," she yelled. "There's a light! Kyanith must be there!"

The mingled excitement and relief in her voice puzzled me. Only a few hours earlier, she had told me that she had talked to Kyanith. No, she had used one of those half-true statements: she had *communicated* with Kyanith. I pulled myself away from the pine support and leaned forward, forcing my right foot to take an upward step and then my left. Within minutes, I saw the yellow glow from the narrow-paned window.

"There's only one light," I told Susan. "And it's dim."

"Of course, it's dim," Susan said. "It's from a kerosene lantern. There's no electricity up here."

"Okay, okay," I said. "Shouldn't you yell, or something? She might think that we're prowlers and shoot us."

Susan giggled, a welcome sound. I felt the emotionally imposed distance between us begin to recede.

"Kyanith doesn't even kill spiders and snakes," she said. "Besides, the only people who know that she's up here wouldn't harm her."

"If you say so."

I felt my shoulders shrug and then tense and I followed Susan across the clearing. I realized that I was anxious and a little afraid to meet Liz's daughter. What if Kyanith, too, blamed me for her mother's death?

Chapter Twelve

Susan was on the bottom step of the porch before she revealed her presence. And then, it was in low, normal tones.

"Kyanith? It's Susan. I'm coming in. I've brought Jackson with me, so get some clothes on."

There was no answer from inside, but then Susan seemed to have expected none. She turned the doorknob and pushed the door open, revealing the sparsely furnished interior of the log cabin. When she walked in, I followed her and closed the door behind me.

"Wait here," Susan said. "I'll go check the loft. She sometimes sleeps up there."

I watched Susan's long legs as she climbed the thick, hand-hewn planks that formed the narrow staircase. I found myself thinking of the months that Papa Gordon and my father, Elmer, had spent lovingly carving thick logs into the warm furnishings of this room.

A hunting cabin, it had been called. Elmer had used it as headquarters when he had mined the Violet Fern. And Liz and Frank had used it for the same purpose. But, judging from the assortment of carvings scattered on the narrow shelves lining the walls, Kyanith must have used it as a studio. I walked over near the rock fireplace, smoked black from considerable use, and looked closely at a carved bird. Kyanith was good, I marveled, as I took the lightweight piece in my hand and traced the delicate etchings that defined the wings. Given time, she would be better than Liz.

"She's not here, Jackson."

I looked up to the square opening in the ceiling corner where Susan stood. Her slumped shoulders revealed disappointment and concern. I couldn't see her face, but her voice was thick with anxiety.

"She probably went for a walk," I consoled, watching Susan carefully pick her way down the stairs. "After all, she left the lamp

81

burning. She can't be very far away."

Susan had reached the bottom stair now and the yellow light illuminated horizontal lines furrowed across her forehead. She smiled. A thin, tight smile.

"Look around here on the main floor," I suggested. "Perhaps she left a message."

Susan nodded. Close enough now to read the defeat in her eyes, I felt a momentary surge of compassion, knowing that, somehow or another, Susan's relationship with Kyanith paralleled the one I had with Marvin.

"I don't know what to do, now," Susan whispered, looking helplessly around the room. "She should have been here."

My fingers ran over the grooves of the wooden bird. Aware of Susan's misery, I moved toward her. She stiffened and stepped back.

"Don't sympathize with me," she warned. "Don't you dare be sweet and supportive."

"Why *not*?"

"Because, I can't afford to relax and let down. I can't be disappointed and cry."

"Again I'll ask you: *Why*?"

Susan shook her head and walked to the north window. When she pulled back the muslin curtain, my unformed questions died in my throat.

"Oh, God," I said.

"Because we don't have that much time, Jackson."

I nodded. It was back. From the vicinity of the Violet Fern, the blue light pulsated with a ferocity greater than previously. Or, was it simply closer, now?

"Susan, we need to talk."

"I know," she said, dropping the corner of the curtain she'd been grasping. The light colored fabric held the crinkle of her grasp. "I know, Jackson."

* * *

"A hundred years ago, Kyanith would have been called a seer," Susan began. "In Puritan New England, she would have been branded a witch. She would have been a druid at Stonehenge."

"What are you talking about? You're saying that Kyanith has extrasensory perception?"

"She is a sensitive," Susan corrected.

"Sensitive, psychic, they're all the same, as far as I'm concerned.

82

I never expected this from you, Susan. I thought you were more level-headed"

"Thanks for the back-handed compliment, Jackson, but whatever makes you think that one can't be both psychic and levelheaded?"

"Have you met Moonshadow?"

"Don't use her as a typical example."

"I don't know Kyanith. Moonshadow is the only person I know who claims to be a...what did she call it, a..."

"A channel," Susan interrupted. "A modern-day interpretation of the old process known as mediumship."

"I don't think I want to know any more about that aspect," I said. "I just want to know what's going on with this mess at the Violet Fern."

"Pull up a chair and sit down." Susan said, easing her body into one of the large chairs beside the fireplace. I followed her example and dropped into the chair on the other side, facing her. Something about the present conversation reminded me of the earlier nightmare down at the creek. I glanced back at the north window; the muslin curtain had muted the electric blue glow to a cool pastel.

"What does it mean, Susan? Tell me about that light at the Violet Fern."

"Jackson, I don't know everything. Probably not much more than you do. Kyanith is the key."

"An emotionally unstable teenager."

"Don't judge, Jackson. Do you consider me unbalanced? Emotionally unstable?"

"You know better than that."

"What about Papa Gordon? Was he crazy?"

"I don't know. I was not in contact with him for the last few years. Before his stroke, no."

"I can guarantee you that the stroke didn't affect his mental and emotional functioning."

"Susan, what point are you trying to make?"

"Just this, Jackson. Your Papa Gordon was psychic. He was clairvoyant, telepathic..."

"Telepathic?"

"He lost the use of his hands after his second stroke. How do you suppose he and Kyanith communicated after that?"

"I didn't know..."

"I forgot. We neglected to inform you of that stroke."

"Sarcasm does not become you, Susan..."

"Damn it, Jackson. You have two choices. You can go back to your posh position in Hollywood..."

"Albuquerque, Susan. I put gasoline in cars and trucks"

"Or," she continued, ignoring my interruption, "you can stay here and help the people who were, at one time, your family."

"I'm here, aren't I?"

"Then I would suggest that when in Rome..."

"I get the point, Susan. I'll take your word that this psychic nonsense is valid if it'll help get things back to normal around here."

Susan smiled sadly. She clasped her hands together in her lap.

"Jackson, did anything ever happen to you that you couldn't explain with logic? That seemingly had no scientific validity? Something out of the ordinary, with no reasonable explanation?"

"Perhaps," I said, thinking of the blue light, of my conversation with Moonshadow, even the strange dream.

"I'll take that answer as affirmative," Susan said. "Just humor me and pretend that you accept. It's the only way I can explain the events at the Violet Fern."

"I'll go along with anything, Susan. Just start talking."

"Something strange happened at the Violet Fern a long time ago."

"Agreed."

"You know about the three men who disappeared at the mine before your father did?"

"I've heard something about it. They were prospecting for gold, weren't they?"

"Correct. A widow of one of the miners sold the property to Gordon. She told him that her husband had wanted to stop digging the tunnel."

"Did she say why?"

"Ghosts."

"Ghosts? Come on, Susan!"

"That was her husband's interpretation of the voices they heard in the tunnel."

Marvin had heard voices in the tunnel. I controlled my desire to tell Susan. At this point, she didn't need reinforcement for her far-out speculations.

"Tell me about the voices," I urged.

"According to the widow, the voices were youthful and spoke in English."

"Kids playing jokes?"

"These were men intent on getting rich, Jackson. They were serious. Don't you think that they would have checked out that possibility?"

"I suppose. What did the voices say?"

"The exact messages have been lost," Susan said. "But, they cried to be released."

I swallowed, in an attempt to dispel the pulsing in my ears. Could it be?

"Susan, have you and Marvin Garland discussed this?"

"Marvin?" Susan asked, puzzled. "I don't think that Marvin is any more eager to discuss the supernatural than you are."

"You would think that, wouldn't you?"

"No one has any proof, but the three men went to the mine one Monday and never returned."

"They could have gone west to more fertile areas," I suggested. "California, Nevada."

"Anything is possible," Susan agreed. "But your father's fate is almost certain."

"Almost."

"What about Liz and Jason?" she asked. "There were several witnesses."

"A landslide," I argued. "There was nothing supernatural about that!"

"Have you talked to Frank and Moonshadow? What did Marvin tell you?"

"I talked to them. It seems that there was a lot of confusion. Nobody is really sure what actually happened."

"What about Marvin?" Susan probed. "You would believe something that Marvin told you."

"Okay, Susan, okay. Marvin thought he heard babies calling to him. But, you have to agree that he was under a terrific amount of stress and pressure."

"Jackson, there's something in that tunnel that has to be released."

"Are you crazy?"

"Perhaps I am."

"There's nothing in that mine! Rocks! Just rocks!"

Susan bowed her head. She squeezed her hands together more tightly. I saw her cast a sideways glance at the north window.

"What do you think is in the tunnel, Susan? Aliens from a flying saucer?"

Her head snapped upright and her eyes burned into mine. She swallowed before she spoke.

"You know, Jackson! You knew all along, didn't you?"

"Dear God, Susan. I was kidding you!"

"We don't have time to tease."

"Do you expect me to believe that there are little people from outer space trapped in that tunnel?"

She continued to stare at me. Still, she said nothing.

"This is a joke, Susan. Am I right? You've all planned this together to get even with me. Correct?"

Susan stood up and arched her back. She gripped her lower lip between her teeth and walked over to the window. With a sharp tug, she pulled the curtain rod from the facing and dropped the muslin and brass to the floor.

"Look at *that*, Jackson!" she cried, a tinge of hysteria coloring her anger. "Do you honestly believe that we created that horrible blue volcano?"

"Calm down, Susan. Remember, this is all new to me. It's as easy for me to accept the proposition that you created the blue light as it is to believe that there are little space creatures inhabiting the tunnel at the Violet Fern."

"It's not space creatures," Susan defended. "How I wish Kyanith were here to explain to you."

"If not space creatures," I asked. "Then *what*? *What* is in the Violet Fern that needs to be released? We'll go and let it out, although I don't know how we can expect to succeed when everyone else has failed. It seems to me that whatever is in the Violet Fern wants to be left alone."

"It's information, Jackson. Information stored there thousands of years ago. It's only now that the time is right to retrieve it."

"Now you're talking like Moonshadow. She actually believes that she has been directed by some supernormal beings to recover certain encoded crystals."

"I agree with her," Susan said calmly. She sat back down in the chair across from me. "Call me unbalanced, unstable, insane. But I have all the proof I need."

"Why haven't you done something about it?"

"Because I *can't*!"

"Well, who *can*?"

"Haven't you stopped to think why you chose this time to come home? After staying away from Arkansas for all of those years, why did you decide to come back now?"

"I have an assignment," I said. "I can make a lot of money if I do that piece on Jace Wright."

"And you expect me to believe that this is the first profitable assignment you've been offered in the last fifteen years? Give me credit for some intelligence. And, some discretion. I know what a good writer you are. You can write anywhere."

"I can promise you that I didn't accept that assignment in order to come back here and open up that godforsaken tunnel!"

"Not consciously, I'm sure," Susan agreed. "But, on some level, you must have known that things here were coming to a head."

"I refuse to accept that."

Susan shrugged.

"Okay," I relented. "I don't believe it but, assuming it is so, what am I supposed to do. I've already told you that I'll try anything!"

She looked at me and shook her head in a combination of disbelief and amazement. A strange sound issued from her mouth.

"You can't do it alone, Jackson."

"You can help me."

"No, I can't. It requires two people whose combined powers are exactly right, perfectly accurate. Otherwise, it will be a failure, like with Liz and Jason."

"*Who*, then?" I demanded. "With whom am I supposed to work to complete this task?"

"Steve," Susan whispered.

"*Who*?"

"My brother. Steve Benson.

Chapter Thirteen

"This time, Susan, you *have* to be kidding."

"No, I'm not."

"Your brother and I working together on *any* kind of project? We can't even get *angry* together!"

"Then you'd better learn quickly how to cooperate," Susan said solemnly. She stood up. "I'm going to try and find Kyanith. Want to come?"

"No, I'll stay here."

"Suit yourself."

I watched her walk out the door and into the eerie bluesparked darkness. I felt the anger first, with the shaking of my hands. Leaving the comfortable chair, I walked over to the curtainless window. The light vibrated with an almost wavelike pulsation. I felt that, if I looked at it from the correct angle, I could see it moving toward me in uniform ripples, like the ones created by tossing a stone into a pool. I had written of this feeling once and I had called my theme "Man Against Nature." In that story, man had won. I searched within my soul for the optimism my hero had shown. I didn't possess it. The feeling of anger faded to one of helplessness.

If I stay around here much longer, I chastised myself, I'll end up just as loony as they are. Marvin and Susan were neurotic, Frank had flipped, and Moonshadow had surely fried her brain years earlier with drugs. I stifled an ironic giggle when I realized that, out of the whole group other than myself, Steve Benson appeared to be the only sane person.

"Damn," I said aloud. "I could use a cigarette."

My words echoed in the near empty room. I patted my shirt pocket before I remembered that I had stopped smoking a year ago. I looked at the two oak cabinets tacked above the makeshift counter. Frank and

Liz had stayed here for several weeks and Frank must have left some cigarettes.

A cursory glance revealed a red tin of Prince Albert and some thin, white rectangular papers. Did I want a cigarette that badly? I did. Picking up the can, I shook it and listened to the rattly slosh that indicated some contents. I grabbed the papers and moved to the pine table on which the lamp sat.

After I had rolled the cigarette, drawing on juvenile memories, I placed it in my mouth, tasting the sharp tang of raw tobacco against my tongue. This is real, I told myself, and I walked over to the counter and opened a drawer, looking for a match. In this primitive cabin, matches were a necessity, both to light the lamp and to build a fire. However, there were no matches in either of the kitchen drawers.

I stared at the kerosene lamp. Through the scarred glass, I observed that the fuel was running low. I sighed. Even this cozy artificial light would be gone before daybreak. I gingerly lifted the globe off and leaned down, allowing the fire that curled up from the coarse wick to singe the tip of my cigarette. Inhaling deeply, I replaced the globe on the lamp and looked at the north window. *The blue light was gone!*

Hurrying over, I peered out, sure that my mind played tricks on me. No, my first perception had been correct. As quickly as it had appeared, the haunting light had taken leave. I rushed out on the porch. The night was normal. Except for the silence.

I hadn't observed the silence earlier, but now I remembered. All the way up the trail to the cabin from the jeep, there had been no sounds other than those made by Susan and me. No frogs croaked, no whippor-wills sang, no owls hooted, no small animals rattled the underbrush as they scurried out of our paths. Those were familiar sounds expected in a summertime Arkansas night. And tonight, they were absent from this vicinity.

I walked over to the edge of the porch and stepped down to the first step. I knew that I should go and look for Susan, but my body seemed drained of energy, lethargic. I dropped to the edge of the porch and sat there, shoulders hunched and arms folded over my upraised knees. The cigarette in my right hand trailed a pungent aroma past my nostrils. I took a final drag and tossed it to the barren earth at the foot of the steps. In the silent darkness, I watched the smouldering butt blink fiery red and then ashy pink.

If I can remember my first thought, I told myself, watching the glare of red slowly shrink to a pinpoint of light, then I can re-think my life and see the wrong turns I made, the detours taken when none were needed. But I couldn't go back. Something blocked those memories from my recall. Struggle as I might, I could remember nothing before the night that Papa Gordon came to tell Mama about my father.

Even though everything up to that point remained blank for me, that night had vividly impressed itself in my memory. I had to have been three or four years old and, because Frank and I had been fussing, Mama had separated us. Having put Frank to bed in our room at the back of the cottage, she had led me to the large bedroom and tucked me into the wide bed that she and Daddy shared.

I could still remember the feathery feel of the down comforter and mattress, the flowery fragrance of Mama, and the slightly oily odor left behind by Daddy. A mentholatum jar between the window and the sill allowed an intermittent breeze to slip through and splash my face.

I could even recall fragments of the dream from which I was awakened. In that dream, I was a graceful bird soaring high above rivers and mountains. In another part of the same dream, I was trapped in a large cylindrical container with round windows. I could look out and see people. I knew these people needed something that I had. I tried to shove it at them through the window, but they couldn't see it.

Papa Gordon's gruff voice had awakened me. Raising my head slightly from the pillow, I had seen him standing in our yard. Someone else had been standing very close to him. It was Mama and she was crying. And Papa Gordon had his arms around her. Although they talked in low tones, I could retrieve pieces of the conversation. Papa Gordon was telling Mama that Daddy was dead.

My child's mind had understood the implications of that statement and I could, to this day, remember the feel of the hot, liquid tears that had squeezed out of my eyes and seeped onto Mama's pillow. I could remember thinking that now Papa Gordon would be my daddy. And I had felt better.

Then they had walked up to the porch and sat down in the swing at the opposite end of the house from Mama's bedroom. The breeze had carried their melodious voices directly to me.

"What happens now?" Mama had asked Papa Gordon. "I tried every way I could to keep him around until Jackson was old enough."

"I know how hard you tried," He said softly. "If ever anyone has given their all, it has been you."

"We could have had those years, Gordon." Mama's voice sounded angry.

"And, in another reality, we do, Sarah. You are the one who reminded me of the fact that this existence is not all that is."

"Why, then, couldn't I have let the *me* from another reality make that decision? Then *that* me would be suffering now, instead of *this* me."

There had been a long silence, broken only by an occasional sniffle from Mama. The conversation had begun to bore me and my eyelids had weighed tons when Papa Gordon had finally spoken.

"In another reality, my love, *this* reality is only probable."

Papa Gordon had moved Mama, Frank, and me into the big house with Mama Kate, Liz, and himself. Liz, at six months, had been a great little toy for me and I had amused myself for hours, playing with her. And then, Mama had died.

Shortly after that, Frank and I began school. And, in such a short time it was over, those schooldays. Frank went to Vietnam and I went to the University of Missouri to study journalism. After winning a literary award and graduating *magna cum laude*, I accepted what seemed to be the most prestigious and lucrative of my many job offers.

Within a year, I had sickened of that position which, in truth, had been that of a ghostwriter for a noted screenwriter. I began work on a novel started in high school and, shortly thereafter, completed *Vindication*. The novel brought me much acclaim and many awards, but little money. My dream to leave the agency was smashed. At that point, I couldn't afford the luxury of unemployment. And, certainly the salary was necessary when I met and married Chris. A tall, elegant, high fashion model, she was accustomed to the best and succeeded in getting it from me.

I was "in love" for approximately eight months. But, it was six years before I grew so unenamoured of both marriage and agency to discuss a divorce. Chris was magnanimous. The only things she wanted from the settlement were the house, the sports car, and the rights to my novel.

Only after I breathed a sigh of relief and signed the agreement did I discover the reason behind her equanimity. Chris had already had a deal in the making in which *Vindication* would become a movie. I allowed my bitterness to poison my whole outlook on life. I lost touch with the people in Bethel Bluff, the ones who had cared for me when I was simply Jackson Cody, without letters, titles, or awards after my name.

At one point in my wanderings, I had decided that anonymity was the key. After all, I convinced myself, the only time that people had unselfishly loved me was before I had become famous. That was when I had begun my trek to oblivion, going from Hollywood to Las Vegas, to Denver, and finally, Albuquerque. And to the anonymity of operating gasoline pumps.

Finally, the circle had been completed. I had returned to Bethel Bluff, to those beloved people, and it was all wrong. They wouldn't let me forget that I had succeeded. And now, they asked me to accomplish the impossible.

Chapter Fourteen

I'm not sure what roused me from my reverie but, at the same time that I heard Susan's voice crying for help, I felt the tremor. Thinking that the cabin was collapsing, I sprang to the ground. The shaking continued. Now I knew it to be a phenomenon I had felt before, an earthquake.

"Susan!" I yelled. "Where are you?"

"Follow the trail!" Her voice sounded weak and was muffled by the roar beneath my feet.

"I'm coming," I shouted, starting blindly toward the area from which Susan's cry had come. I had raced the length of a football field before I realized that I had no idea as to where I was going. I stopped.

"Susan?"

"Over here, to your left. Be careful. There's a ledge of rocks. I'd shine the flash, but the battery is gone."

I followed her voice. Although they were short and choppy, she had spoken several sentences. Perhaps she was not hurt badly.

"Damn," I grunted, feeling my toe numb as I stubbed it. "I found the ledge of rocks."

"Easy now, Jackson," Susan's voice was close now. "Don't step on her."

"Don't step on *her*?"

"It's Kyanith. I've found her and we have to get her back to the cabin."

"Where are you?" I asked, flinging my arms out before me and making a wide sweep. On the second try, I encountered warm flesh and soft hair.

"You've found me, Jackson. Kyanith is right here behind me, on the ground. I couldn't lift her to carry her back."

In the darkness, I felt Susan slide down beside me as I knelt on the rocky ground, feeling for the girl.

"Is she hurt badly?" I asked.

"I don't think so."

Then my right hand touched the bare flesh of a leg. I slipped my fingers around the ankle, searching for a pulse. I had never felt flesh this cold.

"Susan..." I began, helplessly searching for the right words.

"Be gentle, Jackson. I think this has been pretty rough on her."

"Susan, how strong are you?"

"I can't carry Kyanith, if that's what you're getting at."

"No, I don't want you to carry her."

"Then *what*?"

How could I tell her? How could I soften the blow?

"Susan," I hesitated for a moment. "Kyanith is dead"

"No!" she cried. I felt her stiffen. Her sob increased to a scream that threatened to pierce my eardrums.

"Calm down," I cried. "That won't help!"

"She can't be dead!"

"She's cold as a fish, Susan. And there's no heartbeat."

"No," Susan said.

"Yes, Susan. We'll come down in the morning and carry up her body."

"No! No! No, Jackson! Listen to me! Kyanith is in a trance. She's not dead. When she's in a trance, she slows her heartbeat. You just didn't try hard enough. She's in a trance, Jackson. A trance!"

Hoping to avoid a hysterical attack from Susan, I decided to go along with her. After all, I'd been partner to crazier schemes than carrying a dead girl up a mountain in the dark of night.

* * *

After Susan's scream, it took me, at the most, ten minutes to go down the mountain. Climbing back uphill with a hundred pounds of dead weight in my arms occupied the greater portion of an hour. By the time that the dim glow of the cabin window came into view, my arms had gone to sleep and my legs had cannonballs tied to them. Susan ran ahead of me to hold the door open.

"There's a sleeping bag over here by the fireplace," she said. "Hold her a little longer while I roll it out on the floor."

I looked down at the body I carried. Not what I had expected, Kyanith was tall and slender. A woman, rather than a child, the baggy denims and man's shirt did little to disguise wide hips and full breasts. Long, waving, chestnut-colored hair framed a pale face that was a

94

mirror of my own at fifteen. The room spun about. How could Liz's daughter possibly look so much like me? I fell to my knees, holding Kyanith tightly in my arms.

"Susan," I cried. "I don't understand how…"

"You really didn't know, did you?"

I looked up at Susan. She stood above me like some avenging angel, grim face contorted with an emotion akin to satisfaction. Her hands, knotted into fists, hung limply by her sides. Circular patches of red heightened her cheekbones.

"I don't know what to make of this," I said. "I never touched Liz in any sexual way. She was a *sister* to me. How could this have *happened*?"

Susan's large green eyes captured mine. I watched them widen and then narrow into tiny slits as she assessed my face, seeking some answer.

"Susan," I begged, cuddling Kyanith closer to my chest. "Tell me. Please tell me."

At that moment, I felt a flutter of movement from the child in my arms. I loosened my grasp and watched her eyelids flicker. What seemed like a thousand years passed before she opened her eyes and stared at me. Amazement kindled with joy colored her face.

"I knew you would come," she whispered weakly. "I just knew it."

With that, her head fell back on the cushion of my arm and she closed her green eyes. I knew only one person with eyes like that. Accusingly, I looked up at Susan.

"Why didn't you let me know?"

Chapter Fifteen

"*Why*, Susan?"

Ignoring me, she stooped and began pulling at the strings on the canvas bedroll. I looked down at Kyanith. Color had returned to her porcelain-like cheeks and her breathing, still slow, was even.

"Put her on the bag," Susan ordered. "I'll go up to the loft and bring down a pillow and covers. She needs to be kept warm."

I stood up as Susan headed toward the stairs. The burden in my arms no longer felt heavy. My daughter, I marveled. I could have held her feathery weight in my arms fifteen years ago. And all of the years in between. Stories Marvin had told me about Kyanith's isolated, deprived childhood flooded over me and I felt anger and resentment. They had conspired against me, all of them. Liz and Susan. Even Papa Gordon.

The warm, yellow light in the cabin surged to a brighter, more powerful, almost white color. Simultaneous thoughts that Susan had added more kerosene to the lamp and that perhaps this was the last dying light before the fuel burned out completely crossed my mind. I turned toward the table, but it was gone!

In its place stood a highly polished and warmly stained bar with four leather-seated stools. My eyes flickered around the room, futilely searching for the kerosene lamp. The room was different and yet the same. Instead of the two chairs, one on each side of the fireplace, a curving sofa-like structure circled the hearth. A braided rug, oval and basically brown, covered the varnished floor on which I knelt. The kitchen counter, finished in the same stain as the bar, now sported shining steel—or was it plastic?—fixtures. Two metallic appliances, built into the wall near the counter, shone with such high polish that I raised a hand to shield my eyes.

Then I remembered the child in my arms. The baby's tiny head, sprinkled with fine tufts of red hair, rested in the crook of my right arm. Tiny hands and feet flailed the air, kicking and pulling at the white crocheted blanket wrapped around its frail body.

"What the hell?" I said aloud.

The baby looked up at me and gurgled, showing smooth, pink gums. Its eyes, Susan's eyes, stared back at me.

"Susan!" I yelled, rising to my feet. "Damn..."

My voice trailed off into a whisper as I stared at the vision on the stairs. She had changed her clothes and done something different with her hair, but I knew her. The white silk jumpsuit hugged her body with figure-flattering knowledge and her long red hair, brushed to a burnished glow, made a halo around her head. She stepped down another step.

"I'm so glad you're back, Jackson," she said. I watched her moist red lips spread across even, white teeth. "When you found out about the baby, I knew you would return."

"Susan, this is insane! Something's wrong. Where did this baby come from? I had Kyanith in my arms. She disappeared and here is this baby!"

Susan stood so close to me now that I could smell the powdery fragrance of her body, the breath of fresh air wafted by her hair.

"Here," she said, reaching underneath the baby's head and lower body. "I'll take her."

I felt the slight weight lift off my arms as Susan took the baby and held it close, cooing, her breath rippling the thin red curls on the baby's head. The baby reached up a minute hand, grabbing for one of the gold earrings dangling from Susan's ear. Susan leaned her head away and laughed.

"No, darling," she chastised gently. "Mustn't pull Mommy's earring. Mommy needs to look nice for Daddy. She hasn't seen him for a long time."

With something akin to psychological paralysis, I watched the interplay. Was this a dream? It had to be. Susan, wearing the face and body of a coed, looked twenty years younger than she had earlier tonight. And the baby. Where had it come from?

"Come over here and sit down," Susan said.

She led the way to the curving sofa. Dumbly, I followed, slowing only when I looked down at my own body, thirty pounds lighter, and clothed in a blue air force officer's uniform.

"How did you find out?" Susan asked. "Did Liz write to you? I asked her not to do that."

"Why?" I croaked.

"Pride, I suppose," she said, resting the baby across her lap and straightening the delicate coverlet. "Come on. Sit down."

I moved around the back of the sofa and eased my body down on the far edge, nearest the fireplace, in order to look directly at Susan. She smiled.

"I wanted to think that that night in Aspen was as important to you as it was to me," she said.

"Aspen," I repeated.

"Well, Jackson," she giggled, looking directly at me, green eyes sparkling. "Surely you must realize that you made love to a virgin."

I remembered well. My sister's best friend. And I had suffered countless moments of guilt since. But that was sixteen years ago. What did it have to do with this present lunatic situation?

"I named her Kyanith," Susan said, long fingers delicately caressing the baby's head. "It was Papa Gordon's idea."

"Papa Gordon?"

"Have you seen him yet? Of course, you must have. You knew how to pronounce the baby's name. Papa was up here earlier this afternoon. Wasn't it so kind of him to give me this cabin and help me remodel it?"

I nodded. Either Susan was crazy or I was. I began to speculate that we both were.

"Are you going to stay?" she asked. Her eyes held thinly disguised hope combined with apprehension.

"Naturally," I said. Even in a dream, I couldn't hurt Susan, the one woman I'd ever really loved.

Her eyes grew liquid and she again leaned over the baby, placing an index finger in the tiny palm. The baby squeezed her finger in its tiny fist and gurgled again. A surge of emotion I couldn't define rushed through my body. Love, the desire to cherish and protect, the urge to be a permanent part of this family circle. I wanted to take Susan and the baby in my arms and hold them so tightly that we each became a part of the other.

"You don't have to hold her, Jackson. Put her on the sleeping bag. I have the covers now."

Dazed, I turned to the staircase. Susan stood there, still clothed in denim, red hair cropped in a mannish-short utilitarian cut. She held an armful of quilts. I became aware of the weight in my arms. I looked down at a teenaged Kyanith and shook my head.

This whole thing is a dream, I thought, as I gently laid Kyanith on the sleeping bag and then squatted back on my haunches. But, when did it start, I asked myself as I watched Susan pull the covers over Kyanith's still body. Did it start with Liz's death? With that stolen weekend in Aspen sixteen years ago? When I left Bethel Bluff for college? Or, when I listened to Papa Gordon and Mama talk on the porch?

It could have begun, I mused, so long ago that I can't remember. If it did, I thought, and all of this I seem to recall is a dream, then what is my *real* life like? If there *is* a real life. The thought flashed across my mind that perhaps I was simply someone else's dream.

"No!" I gasped.

"What's wrong?" Susan asked. Her startled movement told me that I had spoken aloud.

"Nothing," I said, shaking my head and standing up. I watched her pull Kyanith's sandal off and place it by the sleeping bag. "Just thinking."

"I understand," she said softly, reaching forward to tuck the covers under Kyanith's chin. When she spoke, her voice was muffled. "It kind of makes you wonder about what could have been."

I wanted to kneel down beside Susan, to hold her, and to tell her that I would make things right. But, I criticized myself, how can you promise her that? You don't *know* how to make things right. You never did.

"I'm sorry, Susan. I know it sounds feeble, but there are no words to describe just how contrite I am."

Susan stood up slowly. She brushed her hands on the thighs of her blue jeans and shook her bangs away from her eyes. She held her index finger to her tight lips and tiptoed toward the table. Pulling out a chair, she sat down and I scooted into the chair opposite her.

"I've practiced the same apology," she began. "I've thought of thousands of ways to tell Kyanith the same thing."

"She doesn't know?"

Susan shook her head. She placed her elbows on the table, clasped her hands together, and rested her chin on her tightly folded fingers.

"Why?" I demanded. "Why did you give her up?"

I watched her eyes fill. Her mouth tightened and a bright pink patch developed high on each cheek.

"Do you think it was easy? Do you think it was fun? Or simple?"

"I didn't mean to sound critical..."

"Then tell me what you meant, Jackson. Tell me what you would have done!"

"First of all, I would have contacted the baby's father. Didn't I have some rights?"

Susan's glare fell to the table. I watched twin slender lines dampen her pale cheeks. When she raised her head, her eyes held pain and anger.

"I wanted to be important to you, Jackson. As important as that job in Hollywood. As important as Chris Vining."

"But you *were*. You were always the only woman in my life. Sure, Chris infatuated me, but it was *always* you that I loved."

"Why didn't you tell me, Jackson? Why didn't you make an effort to get in touch with me? After..."

"After that weekend in Aspen? Susan, I wrote you a letter. I told you about my plans."

"I never received it. And I'm not sure that I believe you."

"Have I ever lied to you, Susan?"

"Just by omission."

"Wait a minute..."

"What about Chris Vining? Two months after Aspen, you made the front page of the *Bethel Bluff Herald*. There was a fantastic picture of Chris Vining, clinging to your arm as you gazed adoringly at her."

"That was a publicity shot, Susan. At that time, she didn't mean anything to me."

"You married her."

"Almost two years later," I defended. "Not until I was sure of your rejection."

Susan placed her hands on either side of the glass base of the kerosene lamp. She pushed it off to the left and stood up.

"We need more fuel in this lamp," she said. "I think there's a can out beside the back door. Why don't you go and see? I'll light a candle."

The next busy minutes served to relieve some of the tension between Susan and me. Only when we sat down did I begin my defense.

"Susan, I wrote a letter. No, don't try to stop me. I mailed it. In that letter, I told you how much you meant to me and how I looked forward to a future with you. I told you about the necessity for doing a publicity campaign for *Vindication* and the time involved. If *Vindication* were to be a success, as the editors anticipated, I would be free of the agency and could live wherever I pleased."

I paused for breath. Susan stared at me.

"I asked you to marry me, Susan. That June, I would have been free. I asked you to call me or write me with your answer. If I received no answer, I would consider it a rejection of my proposal."

"I still don't believe you," she said. "Either Liz or I checked the post office every day that spring. There was no letter from you."

"I don't know how to convince you..."

"You can't."

"When I didn't hear from you," I said, "I tried calling. You had no phone at school, so I tried your home phone here at Bethel Bluff. The first two times, Steve answered and warned me away from you. Much later I tried and I talked to your mother. She told me you had joined the Peace Corps. She seemed surprised when I asked if you had left a message for me."

"Why didn't you come back here?" Susan asked. "You could have flown. Or driven. If I had been that important to you, it seems that you could have done more than write a letter and make a few piddling phone calls!"

"Susan, did you ever stop and think that perhaps I was as afraid of rejection as you?"

"No," she answered abruptly. "You were successful, famous. You were rich and handsome. I was a little nothing schoolgirl from a red-necked background."

"Oh, no," I laughed, leaning back in my chair. "Not at all. Remember all of those guys at the lodge I had to fight off when I left you alone by the fireplace? Remember how heads turned when we walked into a room? Those were male heads, not female. Those men had no desire to look at me."

"It could be," she said hesitantly, the hint of a smile warming her face. "I was kind of cute, but I was no high fashion model."

"No," I said. "You had too many curves. Too much intelligence. Too much personality. Susan, how could you have kept from knowing how crazy I was about you?"

"I thought so," she said. "For a little while. But I didn't hear from you. And then I discovered I was pregnant. And, about the same time, the rumors started that you and Chris Vining had something going."

"You didn't give me credit for any depth, did you?"

"There was nothing to prove otherwise. I had no communication from you. And then, when Liz called you..."

"Hold on," I interrupted. "*When* did Liz make the call?"

"She called you the weekend after graduation," Susan said.

101

"Somewhere near the end of May."

"She didn't talk to me."

"Yes, she did," Susan argued. "We were together, in Papa Gordon's study. It was after Mama Kate died and Liz had already been home for a month. I broke down and told her I was going to have your baby. Right away, she took matters in her hands and called you. I was there, Jackson! I heard her!"

"You may have heard *her*," I said quietly. "But she wasn't talking to *me*."

Silence pulsated through the room. Kyanith's soft breathing was the only sound. I cleared my throat.

"I doubt that she was talking to anyone, Susan."

"You think she faked the call? Why would she do that? Liz loved both of us!"

"Remember the personality fragmentation you told me about? The Liz that was Andy, the Liz that was Liz, and the Liz that was Betsy?"

"Yes."

"Didn't you tell me that this occurred near the time of Mama Kate's death?"

"Right after," Susan said.

"Correct me if I'm wrong. The loving compassionate part that cared for you and me was Betsy. And the responsible part that would have felt the need to determine the baby's destiny was Liz."

"And it was Liz who made the phone call," Susan whispered. "It was Liz who made all of the plans to hide me at Gordon's Glen while I was pregnant. She knew that Steve would have killed me if he had discovered the truth." Her voice trailed off and I had to strain to catch the next words. "It was Liz who helped me get into the Peace Corps."

"You'll have to admit it now, Susan." I said. "Liz was crazy."

Chapter Sixteen

The speculations could have gone on for hours as to the reasons for Liz's eccentric behavior but, with the completion of my last sentence, I felt the chair I was sitting on vibrate. I watched the kerosene in the lamp roll from one side to another. As soon as I grabbed the lamp in my hand, the shaking stopped.

"They've been happening more often in the last couple of days," Susan said.

"Earthquakes? In Arkansas?"

"You've forgotten your geography. The New Madrid earthquakes in northeastern Arkansas last century changed the course of the Mississippi River. We're sitting on top of one of the most potentially devastating fault lines in the world."

"Now that you've mentioned it," I said, easing the lamp back to the table's surface. "I do recall studying something about it in sixth grade."

"Good," Susan said, a smile illuminating her face.

"How long have the tremors been going on? I don't remember anything like this when I was growing up."

"Just the last few months," Susan said. "I'm sure that's the reason the state geologists are checking the mining claims around here. I think they feel that the miners are contributing to the instability by using explosives."

"Could an earthquake have caused the landslide at the Violet Fern?"

"That's a very plausible explanation," Susan said. She tilted her head. "Did you hear that?"

"What?"

"That sound. I'm almost positive that I heard voices."

Voices? I could do without any more voices.

"It's Frank!" she cried, jumping up from the table and rushing to open the door. "Frank and Moonshadow!"

I'd never been more glad to hear my brother's voice than I was at that moment. I followed Susan to the door and looked at the two people standing by the porch steps, breathing heavily. Frank's left arm was draped around Moonshadow's slender shoulders and her right arm was around his waist.

"Last time I made this trek after dark," he said. "I had both legs. It was hard, even then." He patted Moonshadow's shoulder. "This little lady has a lot of guts."

"Thanks, Frank," Moonshadow said, sliding out from under his arm.

"And you're strong, too," he laughed. "Here, Jackson. You give me a hand up the steps."

By the time I had Frank through the doorway, Moonshadow and Susan already knelt on the floor by the sleeping girl. They conversed in low tones. I eased Frank into one of the big chairs by the fireplace and turned to watch them. Moonshadow had both of Kyanith's hands clasped between her own.

"She's been under too long," I heard her whisper to Susan. "Was she this way when you found her?"

"No," Susan answered. "Much deeper. Her pulse rate was almost imperceptible. Jackson thought she was dead."

"She did it by herself," Moonshadow said, astonishment evident in her voice. "I didn't think she was ready."

"All of the other processes have speeded up," Susan said. "I suppose we have to assume that her development did, also."

"What are you two talking about?" I asked, sitting down in the chair nearest them. "What kind of development?"

"He doesn't know?" Moonshadow asked Susan.

"I haven't had the opportunity to tell him."

Moonshadow looked at me. She lifted her eyebrows.

"I hope that whatever you did was more fun than talking."

"We talked," Susan said, blushing. "We just didn't get that far. What are we going to do about Kyanith?"

Moonshadow shrugged off her backpack and began rummaging through it. From one pocket, she removed several clear quartz crystals. From another, she took some pink, shrimp-colored stones.

"What are those?" I asked, pointing to the pink stones.

"Those are pink phantom crystals," she said, moving around Kyanith's still body, laying first a clear crystal and then a pink one on the floor beside the teenager. "They're starseed crystals."

My forehead must have worn a banner with the word *ignorant* printed on it. Moonshadow looked at me with surprise.

"You don't *know*?" she exclaimed. Then she turned to Susan. "This turkey and your cretin brother are supposed to save civilization? God help us!"

She rolled her eyes upward. I resisted a base desire to slap the daylights out of this smug, arrogant, decaying hippie. Susan accurately assessed my thoughts.

"Frank, would you like some coffee?" she asked, rising to her feet. "Jackson, you can walk with me down to the spring for water."

"Sounds good," Frank said. "I'd go, but..."

"That's okay," I said. "But I'd appreciate the loan of your flashlight."

"Sure thing," he said, dark eyes twinkling. "You know where I dropped it out on the porch?"

* * *

"Thank you," I said to Susan, as we began the walk down the hill. "If I'd stayed in that room much longer with that pompous bitch, I'd have knocked the shit out of her!"

"I know," Susan giggled. "She does have the tendency to bring out the animal in us."

"Who does she think she is, anyway?"

"The problem is that Moonshadow *knows* who she is and feels a little self-righteous."

"And we don't know who *we* are?"

"Not completely."

"What do you mean by *that* ambiguous statement?"

"Watch it, Jackson! You're going to walk right off the bluff if you're not careful!"

I turned the flashlight to my right. A black chasm revealed itself in the yellow cone.

"Why didn't you tell me that this was an obstacle course? What is Moonshadow doing to Kyanith?"

"It's one of her techniques to help Kyanith come safely out of the trance."

"Does it work?"

"If she thinks it will work, it will."

"Come on, Susan. Are you saying that all we have to do is think something and it happens?"

"I'll put it another way. Kyanith will come out of that trance in a couple of hours."

"So whatever Moonshadow does is unnecessary."

"We won't know now, will we?" Susan laughed, slipping her arm around my waist.

Halfway down the mountain, we realized that we had forgotten a bucket. At that point, we couldn't have cared. Susan and I collapsed in a soft carpet sheltered by underbrush and made carefree, youthful, nostalgic love.

Chapter Seventeen

Susan is the strong one, I thought later, as we lay curled together on the lightly cushioned rocky ground, languid with the aftereffects of passion. Maybe the people around her, the so-called enlightened ones, had a better overall perspective, but I'd put my life in Susan's hands any day, rather than Moonshadow's. I felt my chest heave with a silent snort and Susan raised her head.

"We ought to get back," she said.

"What about the water?"

"Oh, there's a well behind the cabin," she said. "It has a hand pump."

"And there's always a bucket beside it."

"Right," she said, rolling over to her knees and patting the ground around her. "Move your leg. You're on top of my jeans."

I folded my hands behind my head and lay back, watching her pull the unflattering fabric over her clean-lined limbs. Then I sat up abruptly, the realization that I could *see* Susan, even dimly, startling me to total awareness. I turned and looked over the trees, toward the eastern horizon. There, the indigo-streaked black faded to gray. I reached for my own clothing.

"What is it?" I yelled to Susan as I hunched my jeans up over my hips. "What is it that Moonshadow expects you to have told me?"

"Never mind," Susan said, fastening the clasp to her webbed belt. "She'll tell you and you'll enjoy it more from her than from me. Moonshadow is quite theatrical."

I already knew that. I'd experienced Moonshadow's theatrics and I didn't care for them. But, then, I didn't anticipate liking anything I was going to hear in the next few hours.

"Race you up the hill," Susan said, moving toward the trail.

"Forget it lady. I'm over forty and I've just completed a vigorous exercise session."

Susan laughed.

"Okay, oldtimer," she said, wrapping her arm around my waist and matching her step to mine. "You lead the way. At your own pace."

The kerosene lamp was still burning in the cabin when Susan and I reached the hand pump. I watched Frank limp over and open a cabinet. He rummaged around and pulled out a light-colored rectangular container.

"The dirty rascal," I said, watching him place one of the cigarettes in his mouth. "He had those hidden."

"They weren't hidden," Susan said. She fitted a metal bucket under the pump spout and grabbed the metal pump handle. "I could have told you where they were."

I listened to the intermittent slosh of water as Susan filled the bucket. Inside the cabin, Frank walked over to the counter, picked up an aluminum container and poured brown liquid into a cup. Forgotten love for my brother awakened within me. He had known why Susan had made that flimsy excuse about the spring. He had come out here after we left and pumped water for coffee. Memories returned of scores of times he had sensed my discomfort and made departure for me easy.

"I don't think we need any water," I said to Susan, pointing to Frank's silhouette in the window. "He's already made coffee."

"And probably finished off the pot," Susan laughed. "Come on, let's go. You can carry the bucket in and preserve some of your masculine ego."

"I think that I've preserved enough," I told her. I threw my arm around her waist and picked up the handle of the water pail with my left hand. "Do we have to go back in?"

"You know we do, Jackson. We've postponed the inevitable long enough."

* * *

Frank was back in the chair by the fireplace and feigning sleep, his head crooked against the high back. Moonshadow was nowhere to be seen, but Kyanith had awakened and sat, yoga-like, on the sleeping bag, a quilt draped over her shoulders. Her sleep-drugged eyes glimmered recognition when I walked through the door.

"Jackson! I dreamt that you came back!"

When she made no move to rise, I put the water pail on the counter and walked over to the makeshift pallet. Kyanith laboriously raised herself to her knees and held out her arms to me. I knelt down and took her in my arms.

"You've always been my hero," she whispered, her breath warming my neck.

I held her at arm's length and stared hungrily. This morning, she was a child. Her long, russet hair tumbled around her shoulders and over her forehead. Baby fat still clung to her cheeks, but I knew that, someday, those prominent cheekbones would highlight sparkling green eyes and break many a young man's heart. She smiled shyly and I pulled her back against my chest.

"Coffee, anyone?" It was Susan's voice. I released Kyanith and stood up, turning toward the wall to sweep away the moisture from the corners of my eyes.

"Come on," Susan said. "There's about a cup left in this pot. I'm going to make some more if I can get this camp stove pumped up."

"I'll help," Frank said, opening his eyes and reaching for his crutch. "Don't ask Jackson. When we were kids, he broke a lantern by pumping too hard."

"Did he?" Kyanith asked, gleefully clapping her hands together. "Really?"

"I sure did. Although I didn't think Frank would remember."

"Couldn't forget," Frank said. He had stumbled over to the counter now and I could hear the hollow metallic *ping* as he pushed the pump on the fuel tank in and out. "As I remember, that was the night you found the snake in your sleeping bag."

"Only it wasn't a snake," I said

"Yeah, but you sure as heck killed it! That poor frog was flatter than a piece of paper the next morning!"

"You've pumped it enough, Frank," Susan said, setting the coffee pot on a burner. "Now, lets light it."

"Where's Moonshadow?" I asked, dropping into the chair next to Kyanith. She leaned her head against my knee and I patted her head. She turned and looked up at me.

"When I was a little girl, I wanted a daddy to do that," she said.

I jerked my hand away and dropped it on my thigh. What had I been thinking? I had no right.

"I still do," she said, lifting my hand back to the top of her head.

"Moonshadow went up to the mine," Frank said, hobbling back over to the chair opposite mine. "She practices some sort of chanting and howling every morning."

"It's a meditation," Kyanith defended. "She learned it in an ashram in India."

109

"Is that like a bordello?" Frank teased.

"Uncle Frank!"

"You would think she would be hesitant about going to the Violet Fern," I ventured. "There were two earth tremors earlier."

"Oh, she knows that she is safe," Kyanith said, turning to look up at me.

"She *knows*?" I questioned. "That's kind of God-like, isn't it?"

"Moonshadow isn't hesitant about letting you know she's a goddess," Frank laughed.

"We're all gods and goddesses," Kyanith said. "Everyone is. Moonshadow has just forgotten the last step."

"The last step?" Susan asked, pulling a chair away from the table and dragging it over next to Kyanith's bedroll. She sat down. "What does that mean, Kyanith?"

"Moonshadow says that there are seven steps to achieving spiritual perfection," Kyanith explained. "The last step is the one she keeps forgetting. It is made when the individual takes no pride in having achieved the first six."

"You have her pegged pretty good," Frank said. "I wouldn't know anything about it. I'm still on the bottom rung of the ladder."

"That's not so, Uncle Frank. You're highly advanced. That's why you're here. It's why we're all here."

"That's nice to know," I said, half joking.

"You already knew."

I glanced over Kyanith's head, at Susan. She lifted her eyebrows and smiled.

"You refused to acknowledge it," Kyanith continued. "That's why such drastic measures were necessary to get you back here."

"I'm not sure he's ready, Kyanith."

I looked toward the back door. Faintly silhouetted by the arriving dawn, Moonshadow leaned against the facing. She straightened and walked regally toward us.

"My guides have told me that the polarities are not enough to the extreme," she announced.

"Polarities?" I asked.

"Fellow Falcons, I'm afraid we've failed in our mission. Another twenty-six thousand years will pass before the conditions are again perfect. We have not only lost the waiting members of our order, *we have doomed planet Earth!*"

Chapter Eighteen

Good God," I croaked, looking first at Frank and then at Susan. "Does she really *believe* this?"

"And you, Jackson Cody," Moonshadow shouted, pointing a finger at me, "are a major cause of this dilemma!"

I felt my muscles twitch. The only thing that kept me in my seat was the pressure of Kyanith's hand on my leg. I stared at Moonshadow, attempting to assess her for what she was. Knee-length, fringed moccasins covered her feet and legs. Silver bracelets encircled her arms. Gypsy earrings dangled from her ears and her fading blond hair looked as if someone had taken a blowtorch to it. A tall, slender woman, dressed in outmoded, outdated long skirt and embroidered peasant blouse, she managed, by her very stance, to convey a message of authority.

Varying degrees of expectancy reflected from each face as I looked at Susan and Frank, then at Kyanith. They *wanted* me to listen to Moonshadow. I decided, at that moment, to perform one completely unselfish act. I relaxed, leaned back in my chair, and ignored the pointing finger that I so greatly desired to break.

"Take it easy, Moonshadow," Kyanith spoke. "Remember that it's also *our* responsibility. If one of our group is ignorant of the plan, it is because we have failed in our duties."

Moonshadow's eyes widened and she dropped her arm. Wordlessly, she turned and walked toward the kitchen. Her slumped shoulders belied the angry set of jaw I observed in profile.

"Will somebody tell me what's going on?" My words echoed in the hollow silence. "Is *she* the only one who can tell me? The rest of you seem to know. Why can't one of you enlighten me?"

"Moonshadow's function is that of Record Keeper," Kyanith explained. "It was for her to remind you of the reasons we came and why

111

we have gathered here at the present."

"So, she's the head honcho and we're the peons," I said.

"If you wish to think of it that way," Kyanith said, smiling. "Actually, you will discover that your duties are of extreme importance. And, at that time, *you* may be head honcho."

I still had problems with these advanced adult messages coming from the child-like mouth of a teenager. I patted her head again, feeling somewhat foolish as I did so.

"Kyanith is right," Moonshadow said, dragging the remaining chair over to the semi-circular seating arrangement we had formed. "I have a tendency to let my impatience take control when I realize just how little time we have left."

I made a silent vow that I would not interrupt Moonshadow again. But, at the same time I promised myself that, as soon as she finished, I would grab Susan and Kyanith and leave this part of the country. I wished for normal life. I would even smile with grace when a tourist cursed at me for leaking gasoline on his car.

"According to linear time," Moonshadow began, sitting on the edge of the wooden chair, "it began eons ago. On a planet beyond this star system, beyond any star system in this universe, a highly developed civilization dwelt. This civilization had developed intellectually, emotionally, psychologically, and spiritually to the degree that they needed no physical bodies. Actions and deeds had only to be thought and they were accomplished."

I looked at Susan, remembering her earlier explanation of Moonshadow's crystal layout. It will if she thinks it will. Susan nodded her head slightly and smiled. I turned back to Moonshadow.

"Because the members of this civilization knew this ability to create and manifest, there was no conflict among the people. War was a word from millions of years previous. Negative emotions were impossible because these beings had so polarized themselves to the positive that manifesting the opposite end of the spectrum had left their memories.

"Because they concentrated only on the positive," Moonshadow continued, "they were able to consider the negative end of the emotional spectrum only as a gap. Nothing. A vacuum. Do you understand, Jackson?"

"Certainly, I understand the *concept*."

"That is all you need to understand at this moment."

"Susan," Frank interrupted. "The coffee's perking."

"Thanks," Susan said, leaving her chair. "I'll go and turn it down. Please continue, Moonshadow."

"This part may be a little more difficult to comprehend," Moonshadow said, looking at me.

"I'll try."

"Although these beings had no need for physical bodies, they did require a star system, for lack of better words, on which to concentrate their energies."

"I can accept that," I said, matching her stare.

"The star system in which they lived had been manifested and programmed to destroy itself at a given point. These beings had to find another star system."

"Why didn't they just create another one?" I interrupted. "If they possessed this manifesting ability, or whatever you call it, all they needed to do was think of another one."

"Precisely," Moonshadow said. "They concentrated their energies and manifested another star system. A star system with nine planets. Only one of the planets, the third, was capable of supporting the type of life they wished to inhabit it."

"*This* solar system? You're telling me that these godlike creatures manifested Earth?"

Moonshadow nodded.

"And *us*? Do you expect me to believe that I exist only because someone *thought* of me?"

"Susan can explain that better than I," Moonshadow said. "My duty is as Record Keeper. Let me continue with my part."

I nodded.

"Because the beings were no longer physical, they populated the planet with living creatures through whom they could gain experience and expand their consciousnesses."

"If they were so perfect," I protested. "Why did they need further development?"

"One is not perfect until one has learned all that is," Moonshadow said, turning her stare to Susan who had walked back to the circle, carrying a tray with five steaming mugs.

"I can use that," Frank said, reaching for a mug.

Susan held the tray to me and I lifted a mug. Kyanith took a cup and Moonshadow shook her head when Susan passed the tray in front of her. Susan held a cup in her hand and set the tray down beside Frank's foot. He grinned at her.

"Continuing with the lesson," Moonshadow gritted. "The highly advanced beings populated the planet with living human beings who were capable of the emotions that the advanced beings remembered. Are you following me, Jackson?"

"Sure," I said. "They made all of these human beings perfect. They were only good because the super beings didn't remember bad."

"Damn!" Moonshadow cried. "I knew he wasn't listening to me! Why does this always happen to *me*?"

"Moonshadow!" It was Kyanith's voice. "Right now, you're experiencing a very earthly emotion called near-hysteria. This is Jackson's first exposure! Slow down and tell him again."

"Okay," Moonshadow groaned. My right hand itched to toss the remainder of my coffee at her. "Jackson, there are no *goods* and *bads*, only positive and negative ends of the same spectrum. You have to *drop* this idea that positive is good and negative is bad!"

"Consider it dropped."

"I told you that their concentration on the positive end allowed them to *forget* the negative end. Through time, then, the negative end was perceived only as a *gap*, or *vacuum*. Are you still with me?"

I nodded, feeling like the slow learner in a classroom. And I dearly detested my teacher.

"They filled their creations with emotions," Moonshadow continued. "The emotions that they *remembered*. Do you understand, Jackson?"

"Yes!" I barked. "They filled them with positive emotions and *gaps*!"

"You're right!" Moonshadow sounded pleased. "But you know, don't you, that those gaps were not truly gaps."

"They were negative emotions," I said, actually feeling rather proud of myself. And smug.

"Give that man a star!" Moonshadow said.

"You're being pompous again," Kyanith said.

"I'm sorry. I just keep remembering the many times I've tried to remind him."

"What do you mean?" I asked. "This is the first time you've ever mentioned this to me!"

"When I was your mother..."

"My mother! You want me to believe that you were my mother? Sarah Cody? And you've come back in this body? Heaven help us all!"

"Please, Jackson," Susan coaxed. "You've gone along with the rest

114

of it. Try to keep an open mind."

Open mind or not, this had gone a little far. The very idea! I glared at Moonshadow.

"Time passed," Moonshadow continued, ignoring my glare. "The advanced beings realized that their manifestations had not been perfect. The new beings were exhibiting emotions that the advanced beings had forgotten. Negative emotions.

"By the time they realized their mistakes," she continued, "it was too late. The creations themselves had manifested other creatures and beings. The polarity between positive and negative became unbalanced, highly dangerous. The beings who had manifested the star system had not anticipated this possibility. They had not considered that the polarity could become so unbalanced as to cause the planet to tilt on its axis."

"The earth is already tilted," I argued.

"*That* tilt was planned," she said, acknowledging my statement. "The tilt about to occur is not part of the master plan."

"And you propose to do something that will postpone or negate the earth shift?"

"Not me, Jackson. *You.*"

"Me? Why me?"

"There's not much more," Moonshadow said. "Just listen and then my duty will have been performed."

"I've already agreed to that."

"When the advanced beings realized what was happening, they knew they had to intervene. They couldn't take away the negative emotions because they had created them. They had to have a way of *reminding* the new beings of their creators, of the positive end of the spectrum that was inherent in each living creature."

"Sort of like Christianity," I said. "Or, for that matter, any of the world's religions."

"The world religions were a natural manifestation of the seed thought placed by these beings," Moonshadow said. "Organized religion, however, served to further unbalance the polarities because it operated, not from the generation of positive, but from the avoidance of negative action. Religion operated from the root concept of fear."

"Not all religions are based on that premise," Kyanith volunteered.

"I'm just trying to condense this for Jackson's benefit," Moonshadow defended. "You're right, Kyanith. I'll try to be less general in my statements."

Either way, I didn't see that it would make a hell of a lot of difference. I didn't see that this conversation had any purpose or direction.

"The seed thought sent by the advanced beings was not sufficient," Moonshadow began. "So they met in council and decided that direct representatives were needed on that planet. These representatives could remind beings of that star system, but they could not initiate change."

"They haven't done too well at reminding," I quipped.

"You're only chastising yourself," Moonshadow said. "You are one of those chosen representatives. As am I. As is Kyanith. Frank. Susan. And many more of your acquaintances."

"You've lost me. There have been many times that I would have changed events if I could have."

"We manifested vehicles and physical bodies for ourselves," Moonshadow continued, looking dreamily over my head. "There were seven starships. Ours was called Falcon Command because our group of beings chose to manifest the free-spirited body of a bird. Because we had intimate knowledge of the first shift of the Earth on its axis, we chose to come to an area that would be accessible when the time was right to make our presence known."

"Because free will is inherent in the master plan, we were to give these earthly beings every possible chance to themselves balance the polarity. In a sense, we were to sit on the sidelines and coach. But something happened. Something else that was in our memories and that we had forgotten."

"What was that?"

"We forgot that the first shift of the earth would affect our starship," Moonshadow answered. "Eleven of us had left the starship. Reconnaissance, you might call it. We were in the air and suffered only the results of atmospheric vibration. But, our starship was buried under tons of rubble."

"Couldn't you have manifested the debris away?"

"You would think so, wouldn't you?"

"So, you're telling me that the starship is buried at the Violet Fern? And you can't get it out because you've lost your powers?"

"*We* have, Jackson. Ater the Earth shifted, the survivors were predominantly of the positive end spectrum. We weren't needed—yet. The starship crew simply reverted to a dream state and the rest of us chose to experience physical life directly. Now, after thousands of years, we know that it is time to release our fellow crew members so that

116

they can nudge the consciousness of the many spiritually advanced human beings who are inhabiting the planet. Human beings who have progressed to the point that they may teach others of their kind. But, without Falcon Command help, these human beings will not be able to fulfill their purposes."

"Without us, the Falcon Command crew can't be released?"

"Without *you* Jackson. Without you *and* Steve Benson!"

Chapter Nineteen

The warm, humid air fanned my sweaty cheeks and lifted damp hair off my neck. I braced my feet between rocks as I climbed the steep path to the Violet Fern. Having forced myself out of the cabin, I had fled into the fresh air of reality. The thing frightening me most was that Moonshadow's insane monologue was starting to make sense. Or, equally terrifying, perhaps it was just beginning to sound familiar.

I could see the clearing up ahead, about fifty feet, where the miners had always parked their vehicles. Grasping a young pine tree, I pulled myself up another couple of feet. Early morning sunlight sprinkled through the forest and touched me with splotches of warmth. It would be a scorcher today, I thought, as I paused and wiped my forehead.

Why would she attempt making up such an unbelievable story? Power? Why would those as intelligent as Frank, Susan, and Kyanith believe her? Why had I even listened to her? A person must really want to belong, I thought, to participate in the conversation I'd just left.

From halfway across the clearing, I saw the reddish-streaked white gash on the mountainside. The actual pit surrounding the new pile of rubble which marked Liz's and Jason's grave seemed smaller than I had remembered, but the ghastly wound on the mountainside, trailing down to a point where I knew the tunnel to be, frightened me. How much force it must have taken to pull that quartz from its ledge!

I snorted as I remembered Moonshadow's "manifestations. " According to her, *we* would have torn that quartz out with our thoughts. The irony of the situation struck me and I let the bitter laughter flow from my body, echoing back at me from the pit.

By the time the tears burned my eyes, I had dropped to my hands and knees on the hard quartz ledge. The rock, already warmed past body temperature by the summer sun, scorched my palms. I relished the agony, wishing for enough pain to drag me back to reality. Then I felt hands on my shoulders. I turned to look up at Susan. I scrambled to my feet and faced her.

"I didn't want you to see me like this."

"I see you only for what you are, Jackson. A beautiful being with a formidable task ahead of you."

"Is this *real*?" I asked, taking her hand and leading her to the edge of the clearing. There, underneath the pines, someone had erected a bench. We sat down.

"What is *reality*?" Susan answered my question with one of her own. "Is it what we can see and touch? Is it what we can taste, smell, hear?"

"I suppose that's what I've always considered real."

"What about feelings? Like love, hate, joy, fear?"

"They're also a part of it."

"So, reality includes some things other than those you sample with your five senses?"

"I guess it does."

"What about dreams?" she asked.

"When I go to sleep, I dream," I said, searching for the correct words. "The fact that I dream is real, but the events that happen in the dream have no basis in reality."

"Do you experience emotions in your dreams, Jackson?"

"Well, yes. I suppose I feel all ranges of the emotions."

"Yet, you insist that something which is not real can instigate the same emotions that your awake 'reality' does."

"I'd never considered dreams in quite that way," I said. "I've always made an arbitrary separation between real life and dreams. Don't ask me to explain. I just know."

"And yet you're asking me to explain something that I know."

"But you're the one attempting to convert *me*," I protested. "I'm not trying to change you."

"You're *almost* right, Jackson. I'm not trying to convert you. I'm trying to *remind* you."

"Remind me of what?"

"Of who you really are."

"I know who I am, Susan! At least, I knew who I was up to a point about two days ago."

"Go back to your dreams, Jackson. It's easier to understand when you have some comprehension of how your dreams work."

"What do my dreams have to do with this?"

"Tell me some of them."

"What do you mean?"

"You're a writer, Jackson. Give me the basic plot for some of your dreams."

"Okay," I said, stubbornly searching through my memory for some of my most obtuse dreams. "In one dream, I'm walking along a path and some people ahead of me are talking. I feel that I need to know what they are saying. Suddenly, their voices are very clear. I listen to them for a few minutes and when I look down at my body, it is covered with bark. I am a tree."

"Another," Susan demanded.

"I am riding in a car with a friend. He speaks to me and I become aware that he is a different friend and the car is an airplane."

"That's good! Give me another one."

Time for the big one, I thought, and looked at her grimly. If she thinks I'm going to tell her a dream that will, in any way, confirm Moonshadow's theories, will she be surprised!

"I'm watching a group of tiny sailors perform a stage play," I said. "I turn to a friend and comment about their skill. He agrees that they are very good, considering that they are an exotic breed of plant."

I felt a smug expression fit itself on my face. Susan grinned broadly.

"Fantastic! Now, in each of those dreams, you were playing the part of an individual other than this one, the one you are right here. The one that you call Jackson Cody."

"Correct."

"And, yet, when you tell the dream, you say, 'I did,' 'I saw,' 'I felt.'"

"How else could I tell it? The dreams happened to *me*!"

"To *you*, Jackson? Or, did they happen to the character you created to experience the dream?"

"Now, you're playing with semantics," I argued. "My mind created the character. But, he *was* me."

"How's that, Jackson? *How* was he you?"

"He knew everything that I know. He had access to my thoughts, my feelings, my talents. He was me. What more can I say?"

"Did he realize that you had created him? Did he know that he would not exist after you awakened?"

"Of course, he didn't. He had a life that could go wherever he wanted."

"Yet, you tell me that he knew everything you know."

"Damn it, Susan. I suppose the poor slob is going on with his life. I really don't have a hell of a lot to do with it, now."

"Go back to your first dream. When you discovered that you were a tree, did you run around screaming that you weren't a tree? That you couldn't *be* a tree?"

"No, Susan, I just accepted it. It was a *dream*."

"What about the friend in the car who became yet another friend in an airplane?"

"It was a *dream*, Susan."

"Humor me just a while longer," she said. "Think carefully. Do your dream characters know more than you do? Do you know more than they?"

"I told you before. They're patterned after me."

"Like the hero in your book?"

"In a sense."

"Your hero couldn't have taken the car engine apart if you hadn't known how?"

"I had to have an idea of the process. I could have read about it."

"So your fictional characters have to rely upon your background for their actions and behaviors."

"Yeah. I think so."

"And your fictional characters can't do anything that you can't conceive."

"Basically."

"So your dream characters can't do anything that you can't conceive."

"According to your line of reasoning, they can't. But I happen to know damn well that I can't turn into a tree!"

"But you can consider the possibility that reality is far greater than you've thought thus far?"

"Okay, Susan. I'll go back and listen to the rest of Moonshadow's spiel."

"Your dream characters wouldn't like her, either," Susan giggled.

Chapter Twenty

"Susan! Jackson! Are you up there?"

It was Kyanith's voice and, from the sound, originated somewhere between the house and the shelf above the mine where Susan and I stood. We looked at each other and Susan yelled back.

"We're here, Kyanith. we were just coming down."

Kyanith emerged in the clearing a little to the right of the path up which I'd come earlier. Even at a distance, I was aware that she was worried. Her shoulders slumped and she walked as though her feet lacked the desire to move.

"What's wrong, Kyanith?" Susan asked.

"It's Moonshadow," Kyanith said, collapsing on the bench Susan and I had just left. Worry lines creased the smooth flesh across her forehead and her mouth turned down at the corners.

"What did Moonshadow do?" I asked.

Kyanith looked up at me, her expression puzzled. When I spoke again, I softened my tone.

"I'm sorry I ran out, Kyanith. Did Moonshadow vent her anger on you?"

"No, it's not that," Kyanith said, turning and directing her explanation to Susan. "She's doing and saying things that don't fit in."

Kyanith's lower lip trembled and her eyes filled with liquid. I watched Susan's fingers turn white as the girl squeezed them.

"You've got to stop her, Susan."

"We'll take care of her, Kyanith," I said, stepping toward the pair. "Come on, we'll all go back and…"

"No!" Kyanith whispered, turning to Susan. "Don't let him go back! Please!"

"Hey," I said, backing away. "I didn't intend to butt in. I just thought my presence might help."

"She's right, Jackson," Susan said, rising to her feet. She released Kyanith's hands. "This is something I need to do alone. Moonshadow will become more disoriented with extra people around."

"Go ahead," I said, shrugging my shoulders. "We'll stay here. Can I hear you if you yell?"

Susan nodded, her lips tight. She took a step toward the trees. Then she looked back, her eyes searching mine. She seemed to have found the answer she sought. A fleeting smile passed over her face before she turned back toward the cabin.

For silent seconds, Kyanith and I looked at each other. Then she smiled timidly and scooted down on the bench, patting the space beside her.

"What's wrong with Moonshadow?" I asked, walking over and sitting down on the bench.

"It's hard to explain."

"I'll make a real effort to understand."

"Well, she's seeing things that aren't there and talking to people who aren't there."

"Hallucinating?" I asked.

"I suppose a psychiatrist would call it that."

"But you don't?"

"No," Kyanith said. She paused, then added, "It's kind of like being trapped in a dream. A nightmare. You know you're there, but you can't wake up."

"I understand what you're saying. Sounds like a flashback to me."

"It is!" Kyanith exclaimed. Then her eyes darkened. "But you think it was caused by drugs."

Could everyone around here read my mind?

"Only when you allow us," Kyanith said. "Most of the time, we're too polite to let the person know."

"Is anything secret?"

"No," she said, her voice soft with apology. "Nothing. You know it all, anyway. You just won't remember."

I walked away from her, toward the ledge overlooking the tunnel. Each of them, at one time or another, had used the same phrase, indicating that I knew everything that they did, but that I refused to try and remember. It must have been easier for them, I told myself, because I sure as hell had tried.

"Kyanith?"

"Yes?"

I stifled the urge to flinch. I hadn't realized that the girl had moved to a spot almost directly behind me.

"Have you ever lived around ordinary people?" I asked, turning to face her. "Have you ever had a normal friend? Have you gone to a football game? A dance?"

"Come on over here," she said, grabbing my hand and leading me back to the bench. "I want to tell you a story."

"A story?"

"About a little girl who grew into a young woman—with no emotional stress."

"You?" I asked, sitting down.

Kyanith nodded.

"But you were upset a few minutes ago," I protested. "About Moonshadow. As a child, you were deprived of a family, love..."

"Did you ever wish that you could live life over while still retaining all of the information you had gained from living this life?"

"Several times," I answered. "But there are a couple of years I'm not sure I'd want to live over, even with all of the information I have."

Kyanith grinned. Again, I was reminded of Susan.

"You see, Jackson. I came into this life remembering."

"Remembering *what*?"

"My last life."

For a moment, I had almost forgotten that this child/woman sitting beside me was one of *them*. I had almost treated her as a normal teenager. I stared at her.

"Even as an infant," she continued, "I had access to all of the information I had collected and the lessons I had learned in my previous life."

"There's no way I can refute anything you tell me."

"You're right," she said. "But, I can prove it."

"How can you possibly hope to prove such a nebulous concept?"

"Who taught you how to swim?"

"Mama Kate."

"After your mother died, who held you nights when you awoke crying?"

"Mama Kate did. Wait a minute. Are you trying to tell me that you were *Mama Kate*?"

Kyanith nodded.

"Girl, you're crazy! I don't deny that you might really think that you were born as a reincarnated version of Mama Kate, but you can't hope to convince me!"

She smiled, another smile that reminded me of Susan. Why was it that when women had no rebuttal, they always smiled secretively?

"Come on, Kyanith. You heard those stories from Liz or Frank. Or, even Marvin or Susan."

"No, Jackson. I know that explanation is more palatable to you, but it's simply not the case. And, you must stop this denial!"

"This denial, my dear child, is the only thing that allows me to keep my *sanity*!"

"Do you remember a picnic with Mama Kate when you were eight? Just you and Mama Kate. You went to the river and to the Indian mound."

"Yeah," I said. Who could have told her about that picnic? Papa Gordon had taken Liz and Frank with him to Hot Springs to visit a distant relative who was passing through. I hadn't been able to go because I'd been running a low-grade temperature for a day or so.

"Remember what you buried?" Kyanith said, standing up and reaching in her right pocket. She pulled out a small, quarter sized, smooth bluish-black rock. She held it out in her palm and I could see the lighter lines carved by a childish hand.

"It's a star," I said. "And my name is carved on the other side. I don't know how you found that."

"I helped you bury it. Surely you remember that!"

I shook my head. Mama Kate would never have told anyone the secret I buried with that stone. I glared at Kyanith. Would she know the answer to my next question?

"What did I bury with that stone?"

"The one personality trait that you're still fighting," Kyanith said. She took my right hand in her left one and pressed it against her soft cheek. "You buried your fear, Jackson. Your fear."

She had known the answer. Only Mama Kate had known the answer. I would have to accept the possibility that, in her most previous life, Kyanith had been Mama Kate. But I didn't have to believe it.

* * *

"Do you remember why you were afraid?"

My head tingled and my mouth felt cottony. Pulling my hand away from her cheek, I stood up, turning my back to her.

"I remember," I told her. "But, why don't you tell me?"

"It started with your dreams," Kyanith said. "You became afraid that you wouldn't be able to come back to real life, to this life, that you would stay in that dream world forever. You had reached the point that you were fearful of sleeping."

"I had forgotten," I said, turning back to face her. "Every time I felt myself drifting off to sleep, I would sit up, turn over, or force myself awake."

"As if, by giving in, you would be drawn up into a swirling funnel of nothingness?"

"That's what I told her! That's what I told Mama Kate!"

She nodded.

"You could have read my mind. You did it earlier."

"You can believe in telepathy, but you have doubts about reincarnation," Kyanith surmised. "Well, that shows some progress."

I rushed over to the bench and pulled her to her feet. Taking her by the shoulders, I shoved her to the middle of the clearing. Bright sunlight beat on my back and I felt a rivulet of perspiration trail down along my spine.

"Look at that," I shouted, pointing to an enormous oak tree on the hill above the landslide area. "*That's* real! That white streak up in the sky? The shiny speck at the end of it? That's a jet airplane! *That's* real!"

I felt her shoulders tremble underneath my palms. Releasing her, I reached down and picked up a handful of rocks and crumbly soil. I held it toward her, letting the particles sift through the spaces between my fingers.

"*This* is real, Kyanith."

My next statement caught in my throat when I looked at her. Liquid trailed down her cheeks and her eyes were dark with fear.

When I reached for her, she stepped away.

"I'm not going to hurt you," I said.

"I know," she whispered.

"I only wanted to explain."

She nodded.

"I'm sorry. What did I say to hurt you so?"

"It's not what you said," she began. She lifted the long tail of her shirt and wiped her cheeks. "It's what you *felt*."

"What I felt? Explain that!"

"Jackson, I have this ability, talent, or whatever you wish to call it. Sometimes, it's almost a curse."

"Go on."

"I pick up on your emotions."

"I've known people who do that," I said. "But, I've never made one cry."

"I don't stop with sensing emotions, Jackson. I *feel* them."

I remained silent. At this point, what was there to say?

"Just a few seconds ago," she continued, "I experienced your fear, Jackson. I *lived* it."

I moved toward her and she slipped into my arms. I held her, feebly attempting to comfort her.

"It was horrible," she said, her words muffled against my chest. "Your fear was the most painful emotion I've ever felt."

I held her tightly. If she had experienced what I had felt, then she was right. Nothing could be worse than fear.

Chapter Twenty-One

The sun had moved enough to slip the bench into the sunlight, so Kyanith and I moved toward the shade, toward the trail to the cabin. I kept my right arm around her shoulder, allowing myself to feel, for a moment, the pride of fatherhood. A thought kept teasing me, trailing across a corner of my consciousness, and then fading away. When I captured it, I stopped abruptly.

"Kyanith?"

"Yes?"

"You told me that you came into this life aware, knowing everything from Mama Kate's life. Did you know... "

She pulled away and moved to the trail's edge, where she leaned against the trunk of an ancient hickory tree. She looked at me through narrowed eyes.

"I've always known that you were my father, if that's what you're trying to ask."

"How?" I asked, my heartbeat increasing. "I didn't tell Mama Kate..." I hesitated, comprehending. Kyanith's eyes held mine.

"You tell *me*," she ordered. "Tell me how I knew."

"Susan," I said. "You picked up the information from Susan."

"You're beginning to use your talents, Jackson," she said.

I felt the tightness in my chest leave as she smiled. "Actually, I had Mama Kate's knowledge of your love for Susan. I knew Susan's feelings of guilt, rejection, hope, and love. As I grew, I sensed Papa Gordon's knowledge. And Liz's."

"What about the months between?" I asked. "The time that elapsed after Mama Kate died and before you were born?"

"I have vague memories about those times," she said. "But they are becoming plainer now. I know it was a good period, full of love and surrounded by like beings."

"Like beings?"

"I say *beings* because I don't know a better word. It was as if each person, on making the transition from this life to the in-between life, lost her or his body and just became a complex of emotions and thoughts. I use *like* because we seemed to all belong together. Our thoughts and emotions were very similar and we had many, many shared memories."

An old stump beside the trail caught my eye. I moved over and sat down on it, facing Kyanith. Actually, a between-life existence was as easy to accept as most of Kyanith's earlier disclosures.

"How could you have had a normal childhood, knowing all that you did?"

"What's a normal childhood? Look at it from an outsider's point of view. Growing up with Liz's eccentricities and Papa Gordon's incapacities didn't provide the healthiest of atmospheres. Looking at it from my point of view, being rejected by both parents couldn't have been good for development."

"God, I'm sorry."

"Don't chastise yourself, Jackson. I had an *overall* point of view. I knew it was all part of a greater plan. I didn't have to learn the fears, inhibitions and behaviors that most children have forced on them. I had already discarded those characteristics in another life."

"I'm trying to understand, Kyanith. You tell me all of these things and I could write them in a story. I could use symbolism and analogies and probably win an award. But, getting right down to it, I just can't see you as Mama Kate."

"That's because you're looking at physical bodies," she said, walking over to where I sat on the stump. "You see me as a fifteen year old combination of cells that you and Susan supplied. You see Susan's eyes, some of Liz's mannerisms, and your stubborn chin. You have to think of what I was before this genetic possibility came into being. You have to think of what I will be when it ceases to exist."

I looked up at her, trying to see her eyes, but the sun was behind her now. Instead of Kyanith, the fifteen year old, I saw a tall, black, featureless being, light melting the edges of its shape into a parallel series of lines resembling a polygraph reading. I blinked my eyes and shook my head, but the image remained the same. It could have been Mama Kate *or* Kyanith. It could have been neither. It could have been both. Then she moved and the light flooded over her body, returning it to three-dimensional portrayal. My breath came more easily.

"I can tell, by looking at your face," she said. "You're beginning to realize."

"Realize what?"

"That reality is, indeed, more or less than what you experience with your five senses."

"I don't know if I even comprehend what you've just said, Kyanith. How can I hope for more?"

"Think about this," she said, dropping to her knees with a fifteen year old's grace and ease. "Think of a rainbow. What *is* a rainbow?"

"It's an image seen by our eyes," I answered. "It is caused by sunlight passing through water droplets and separating white light into the colors of the spectrum."

"Have you ever passed *through* a rainbow?"

"Of course, I haven't. I could never get that close."

"*Why*? Couldn't you walk that far? Or, drive that far?"

"It's not entirely a matter of distance, Kyanith. All sorts of factors enter into the picture. Say that I decided to walk toward a rainbow. While I'm walking, the sun is moving, the earth is moving, and the water itself is evaporating. When I get to the point at which I estimated the rainbow to be, it probably is no longer there."

"It disappeared."

"You could say that."

"Because you could not see it, it no longer existed."

"I didn't say that, Kyanith. I said that the correct combination of factors necessary for its existence was no longer present at that point."

"It moved?"

"Possibly."

"Try it from another point of view, Jackson. Suppose you could divide yourself in half and a rainbow has formed under ideal conditions not too far away. One half of you stayed to watch the rainbow. Call that half Jackson One. The other half, Jackson Two, is going to walk toward the rainbow. Jackson One will direct Jackson Two, telling him to move right or left, to go backward or forward."

"What about time?" I ventured. "It will take time for Jackson Two to get to the rainbow. The moisture could evaporate. The sun could set."

"You're deliberately being dense," Kyanith accused. "If you can separate yourself into two parts, can't you make time stand still?"

"That's not very scientific."

"And yet you believe that Einstein followed a tiny particle around the entire universe?"

"I get your point. I'll omit time as a factor."

"Now, let's assume that the feat has been accomplished," Kyanith said. "Jackson One has directed Jackson Two through one end of the rainbow and the two Jacksons have reunited. Jackson One saw Jackson two go through the rainbow, so he *knows* the fact to be so. Jackson Two, who did the traveling, didn't *see* the rainbow, so he *knows* he didn't go through it. He also knows that Jackson One is crazy and hallucinated the whole thing. Which Jackson is correct?"

"Jackson One is right," I said. "From his standpoint. After all, he *saw* it."

"Seeing something makes it real?"

"That seems to be what I'm saying."

"And, since Jackson Two didn't see the rainbow when he walked through it, then it is *not* real?"

"From Jackson Two's standpoint," I agreed, "the rainbow was not real because he didn't see it."

"Now, merge the two Jacksons back together," Kyanith instructed. She waited a moment. "Did Jackson Two walk through the rainbow? Was there even a rainbow?"

"Come on, Kyanith. You and I know that the rainbow existed. We created it, along with the two Jackson halves who played with it."

"Good point, Jackson. Think about it."

Think about it? It was like a short story plot or, as Susan had pointed out earlier, a dream. I had created characters, settings, events, experiences. My characters had developed and grown. Were they real? Were the events and experiences real? When one of my characters developed an insight, was it his growth or mine? Did these fragments cease to exist when I no longer thought of them?

"Who are you? What are you doing here?"

I jerked my head up to observe the man standing off to my left a few feet. Tall and rangy, brown hair fading to gray, his hazel eyes, more than the chest-length beard, caught my attention.

"Do I know you?" I asked, trying to discern why he seemed so familiar. He wore faded denims, stained with red clay, typical clothing for a crystal miner. Gummy mud stuck to the soles of his work boots and a portion of a dirty sock stuck out of an inch long slash on the small toe area of his right boot.

"I had a pair of boots like that," I ventured, uncomfortable with his silence. Where had Kyanith gone?

"I cut these with an ax on a camping trip," he said. "Almost took my toe off."

Now I was really uncomfortable. Six years ago, in the Canadian wilderness, I had almost developed gangrene from an ax cut on my right foot.

"Were you chopping wood?" I asked.

"Sure was," he said, moving closer and staring at me. "It was twenty years ago, in Saskatchewan. I kept the boots because they remind me of how lucky I was."

"Lucky?"

"Yeah," he said, frowning. "I had my foot braced on the log and I happened to look up and see this rainbow…"

"Who *are* you?" I demanded, rising to my feet. "Who do you think you are, coming here with my past and my memories?"

"I know who I am," he said. "But I don't know you."

His eyes darkened and he backed away from me. He lifted up his right hand as if to physically hold me at a distance.

"Tell me who you are!" I demanded, taking a step toward him. "Where did you come from? What are you doing here?"

He stood straighter and his head came erect. I had seen Papa Gordon stand like that a thousand times. A stance of authority.

"I live here," the man said. "I own a cabin down the hill a ways and I mine crystals. I haven't always done that. I used to write novels. That all changed after that Canadian trip."

My legs felt weak. I wanted to sit down but, with this man, I needed to stand. I needed to face him, eye to eye. I needed to know what had happened on that camping trip.

"Why did you stop writing?"

"That Canadian trip was a celebration," he said. "I had just ended a marriage with a Hollywood starlet and, after spending several days pitying myself, I had intended to leave camp the next day and go back to work in Los Angeles."

I swallowed. The man standing before me was flesh and blood. He was no figment of my imagination. He was as real as I.

"What caused you to change your mind?" I asked, knowing the answer and yet wanting to hear it from him.

"Well, friend, when I saw that rainbow, I just dropped the ax and started walking."

"And?"

"I walked right through that rainbow. It changed my life."

Chapter Twenty-Two

I closed my eyes. It couldn't be. There was no possible way that the man could be me, even a fragment of me.

"Why not?" It was Kyanith's voice.

"Where have you been?"

"Right here beside you, Jackson. You just didn't see me."

I stared at her and then back at the space where the man had stood.

"You couldn't see me," Kyanith giggled. "So I guess I'm not real."

"Cut that out," I snapped. "There was a man..."

"I know. I saw him."

"It was strange. As if he *had been* me, or *is* me, or *could be* a part of me."

"I know."

"But his Canadian trip," I protested. "It was twenty years ago. I went to Canada six years ago."

"Did everything else seem real?"

"Yeah. Even the part about the rainbow. Only I didn't go through it. I just stood and looked at it."

"It seems that you might have to modify your concept of time, Jackson. Perhaps time has no place in reality."

I snorted. Reaching for her hand, I pulled her to her feet. When this was all over, I would see that my daughter had the best psychiatrist possible. I looked at the sun. It was almost directly overhead now.

"Susan has been gone a long time," I said. "Should we go on back to the cabin?"

"I want to show you something," Kyanith said, pulling me back toward the mine. "Then we can go."

"Wait," I said, holding my ground. "Explain one thing to me."

"Sure, I'll try."

"If that man was me, or vice versa, why did he look like Papa Gordon?"

133

"Jackson, look in a mirror occasionally. Haven't you observed that *you* look like Papa Gordon?"

"No," I said, taken aback. The thought had never occurred to me. "Why should I look like Papa Gordon?"

Kyanith wrapped her arm around my shoulders. She looked into my eyes.

"Because you are Papa Gordon's son."

*   *   *

"Papa Gordon? My *natural* father?"

"Sure."

"I don't understand."

"Come on. Walk with me and I'll explain."

She led me around the edge of the pit and to a stone staircase which looked as if it had been carved out of solid quartz. It led directly to the landslide area and disappeared underneath a large white boulder.

"You won't be harmed," Kyanith said, sensing my reluctance to go any farther. "Just walk carefully. These steps were made for smaller feet."

"I think I know some of the story," I said. "My mother and Papa Gordon were to be married, but Elmer Cody came along. I just couldn't imagine why she married him when she loved Papa Gordon. It's even more difficult now, knowing that she was pregnant with Frank and me."

"Watch this next step," Kyanith said. "The edge is crumbling. I don't know the specifics, but Elmer Cody had a purpose to fulfill and Sarah was the only person who could keep him here."

"A lot of good her sacrifice did," I said, remembering Mama's conversation with Papa Gordon on the night that Elmer had died. "He only stayed long enough to mess up everybodys lives."

"Perhaps that was his purpose," Kyanith said. "Careful, now. We have to get off the steps and walk around the edge of the slide area."

"I'm not sure I want to go there," I said, bracing myself on the bottom step.

"You're okay," Kyanith said. "Liz and Jace were attempting something they weren't prepared for. They were creating a dissonance and it was only logical that they be quieted."

"A *dissonance*? *Quieted*? Isn't that kind of a mild word for what happened to them?"

"Susan can tell you about that. When she explains, you'll understand."

"Don't count on it," I said. "Just tell me in plain English what Liz

134

was doing at the mine. She knew the stories as well as any of the rest of us. She knew the risk involved."

"You're absolutely right," Kyanith said, sitting on one of the stone steps. "She knew it all, but she felt she had to take the chance. Liz knew that you were her half brother. She discovered the truth when she came up here to the cabin after my—pardon me—after Mama Kate's funeral. She found the records in the family bible. Over the years, she built up a fair amount of resentment. Emotionally, she was not capable of very much bitterness. Or happiness, either, for that matter."

"Why did she resent me? We grew up like brother and sister."

"But now, suddenly, you were as much a part of Papa Gordon's life as she was. You were not only *treated* as a son, you *were* a son and, as such, could legally claim a share of Papa Gordon's estate."

"I don't see why that should have affected Liz. I wouldn't have pulled my share out from under her."

"On one level, she knew that. On another level, she remembered similar rivalries between the two of you over the last thousands of years. And this time she was determined to win."

"Why would she do it this way?" I asked. "Opening the Violet Fern? It was the height of insanity!"

"Liz remembered just enough to be dangerous. She knew that the polarities must be perfectly balanced before an effort could be made. She also remembered that the only beings who balanced perfectly were a *Twin Soul.*"

"So Liz and Jason were a Twin Soul," I concluded. "My God, does that mean…"

Kyanith stepped away and looked at me. Despite the sadness on her face, her eyes reflected mirth.

"Yes, Jackson. That's what it means. Steve Benson is the other half of your Twin Soul."

Chapter Twenty-Three

If someone had told me a week earlier that I would be listening to this hogwash, even going along with it, I would have dismissed their ravings as lunatic. But, even as Kyanith spoke the words, I felt them strike home. Still, I felt the need to protest.

"How could Steve Benson and I be a Twin Soul? We don't have anything in common. Absolutely nothing!"

"Moonshadow can tell you about polarities, Jackson. I understand, but I can't explain it very well. Come on, it's just a few steps more."

"I knew a man who met a lady while he was vacationing in the Virgin Islands," I said, slipping on one of the loose rocks at the edge of the slide. "She was everything he'd ever imagined he wanted. They fell madly in love."

"Get to the point, Jackson."

"He told me that he had met his soul mate," I said, reaching for a handhold. I dislodged another large rock and it rolled toward my feet, trailing a small avalanche of pebbles and loose earth. "This guy explained that she was the other half of his Twin Flame. That he was only fulfilled when he was with her. Without her, he was nothing."

"That stands to reason," Kyanith said, jumping from the loose rock of the slide area to a smooth, shadowed patch of ground. She turned and looked expectantly at me.

"Kyanith, he was madly in love with his other half. Steve Benson and I are complete opposites. We hate each other. I couldn't possibly feel the way about Steve that this fellow felt about his lady."

Kyanith smiled.

"Don't smile at me, Kyanith. I do believe that this is the most ridiculous of your postulations. It's so stupid that anyone with a lick of sense would see right through it. And all of you are insisting that it is so!"

"Come on, Jackson. Stand right here beside me. Now, look off just a little to the left. What do you see?"

She had done it. I stared at the large, gaping hole. Waves of an unnamed emotion flooded over me. Kyanith had led me to the Violet Fern tunnel!

* * *

"Don't be afraid," she cautioned. "We're too close together. I'll pick up your fear."

"Don't worry about my fear," I gritted. "Just beware my anger. Why didn't you tell me that the damned thing was still uncovered? I thought that the landslide had closed it off!"

"You never asked," she said, leaving my side and walking toward the ragged opening.

"Wait for me," I yelled. "I'm going with you."

"Aren't you afraid that you'll die?" she challenged, turning back to face me, eyes grim, hands on hips.

"The way that life has been unfolding the last few hours," I said, walking toward her. "Death has to be simpler."

She smiled. Then she nodded.

"You're okay, Jackson."

By the time that we reached the opening, the temperature had dropped a good thirty degrees. I began to sense the dank, mildewy smell of an enclosed area left damp. Memories of the old root cellar at Gordon's Glen flooded over me.

"Stop here," Kyanith ordered.

"Why?"

"Just stop," she said. "Oh, you did it. Sorry, I tried to warn you."

"What the hell?" I asked. I rubbed my stinging nose. Something had hit me right across my nose. Or, I had hit something. I gingerly reached my right hand forward. It met with a solid, invisible barrier.

"It's the force field," Kyanith said, a giggle underlying her words.

"Damn," I said, rubbing my hand over the smooth surface. "It's just like glass, except my hands don't leave prints."

"It's stronger than steel," Kyanith said. "Liz and Jace tried to break through it. Elmer Cody tried."

"And the three mysterious miners," I added. "Don't forget them."

"Do you think you can do it?" she asked.

"Do *what?*"

"Dissolve the force field," she whispered. "You and Steve have to find a way to remove it."

"Tell me what is so important inside this tunnel that this thing has to be destroyed," I demanded.

"You can see them if you look carefully," Kyanith said. "Get as close as you can and squint your eyes."

I moved forward, bumping my forehead this time. The shadowy walls of the cave leaned inward and I could see nothing.

"It's just a tunnel, Kyanith. An empty tunnel."

"Look again."

When I did, I felt the breath catch in my throat. My heart pounded madly and I felt moisture accumulate on my palms. I blinked and made an attempt to focus my eyes, to negate the image I was receiving.

"You see them, don't you? *Jackson*?"

I swallowed and pulled myself away from the invisible wall. I turned to Kyanith and, when I spoke, my voice thundered in my ears.

"I saw them."

"Well?"

My head felt as though giant hands squeezed it. I felt my skin alternately grow warm and then icy cold. Tiny prickles of something akin to electrical shock ran over the skin of my bare arms.

"Kyanith, what in God's name *are* they?"

"What do *you* think?"

"They look like gigantic flat crystals," I said, trying to control the quiver in my voice. "Giant tabular crystals with chevrons lined up inside them." I paused for a moment, remembering Marvin's description. "Probably seventeen chevrons."

"Great!" Kyanith exclaimed, clapping her hands together.

"But, Kyanith," I began. Then I stopped. Where were the words I needed?

"What is it?"

"They moved, Kyanith. They can't be crystals. Those things in the tunnel are *alive*!"

Chapter Twenty-Four

Kyanith, sensing my fear, kept a distance between us as she led the way back to the cabin. Despite my mental befuddlement, my feet seemed to have a clear idea as to where they were going. Neither Kyanith nor I spoke a word on the way out of the pit and down the mountain to the cabin. Susan met us at the door.

"My God, Jackson," she cried, when she saw me. "Your hair! What has happened?"

I shook my head, still incapable of speech. Susan placed her palms on my cheeks.

"Kyanith," she cried, eyes flickering about the clearing, searching for her daughter. "Kyanith, come and help me!"

"What's wrong out here?" Frank yelled, clutching the railing as he limped down the porch steps. "What's everyone screaming about? Holy shit, Jackson! What happened to your face?"

I wanted to stop shaking. I willed my body to quit trembling. Fear coursed through the icy veins and arteries of my body. Fear, not of the things in the tunnel, but fear of the unknown. I knew where I'd been and I thought I'd been at the bottom, but I had experienced no terror to compare with this madness. I had been correct earlier when I had told Kyanith that death would be simpler. Despite the thundering of my heartbeat, I heard Susan's voice.

"Frank, help me stretch him out. Watch that rock! Easy, now."

"God," Frank groaned. "It's terrible. He's aged twenty years. What caused it?"

"Shut up," Susan said. "He can hear you. Moonshadow, please go and get Kyanith. She's up there somewhere in the woods."

I felt something soft being shoved under my head. I tried to grunt my gratitude. Frank answered.

"That's okay, brother."

Then I felt the wave of air as a figure scooted down beside me. Strong hands pressed against my temples, weaving circular threads. I felt the fear being pulled from me. No longer did the black funnel threaten to tow my soul into oblivion. Kyanith's face came sharply into focus. Tears coursed down her rigid, white cheeks. Eyes closed, she moaned. The soft groan grew into a wail, and then a scream.

"Enough, Kyanith," Moonshadow cried, pulling the girl away. Kyanith gasped and struggled to pull herself to a sitting position. She reached for my hand.

"You've taken enough of his fear," Susan said. "If you continue, you'll destroy yourself."

Kyanith seemed to comprehend. She quit struggling and turned over on her side, breathing heavily. I watched her shivering slow, and then subside.

"Jackson?" Susan asked, patting my cheeks with soft hands. "Can you hear me?"

"I hear you," I said, trying to raise my head. Failing, I let it fall back on the fabric Frank had tucked underneath my head.

"Are you satisfied, now" Moonshadow asked, her sarcasm directed toward Susan. "We have two of our most strategic members disengaged. Are you pleased?"

"That's enough," Frank said, his voice harsh. "We've humored and placated you, Moonshadow. We've each gone out of our way to pacify you. We've allowed you to swell up with your own importance, sure that you would realize how utterly stupid you were behaving."

"I..."

"Don't interrupt me," Frank shouted. "Don't you remember humility? Unconditional love?"

"But..."

"And I'm not interested in that pious, holier-than-thou attitude about all of the sacrifices you've made to get us to this point We *all* have sacrificed! Each in his own way!"

"Frank," Susan interrupted. "Kyanith is trying to conquer fear. Don't compound it by giving her anger to deal with."

"You're right, Susan," Frank said, his voice softening. "Look, Kyanith seems to be coming around."

I turned my head, feeling the scratch of a plastic button against my cheek. To me, Kyanith appeared the same as she had a few minutes earlier, still and quite. I watched her hand move, fingers stretching and then folding into her palm. Then her entire arm moved and she turned over on her back. Her eyes opened. I felt a stinging breath pass between my lips.

"Jackson," she whispered. "Is he…"

"He's fine," Susan said, moving over to Kyanith. "You saved him, darling."

"Susan, I was terrified!"

"I know, sweetheart," Susan said, taking Kyanith's hand in hers. "We can all see what it did to the both of you."

* * *

Afternoon sunlight had warmed the cabin to a distasteful temperature by the time that the five of us had recovered enough to assemble again. After a short discussion, we all agreed to sit on the ground underneath a large elm tree in the front yard. Susan and I leaned against the trunk of the elm tree and Kyanith sat to my right, legs folded in her semi-yoga position. Moonshadow, sitting in the middle of our lop-sided circle and considerably humbled by Frank's criticism, apologized to the group.

"I've been informed," she said primly, "that I've overreacted somewhat and, if that is the case, then I want you all to know that I'm sorry."

Frank, reclining against the bottom porch step, looked at me and raised his eyebrows. He rolled his eyes and I smiled. I wished I were man enough to go over and put my arms around him. It was good to have my brother back.

"Now that the polite part is over," Moonshadow continued. "Time is short and we need to get on with the plan."

"I think we've all agreed on that aspect," Susan said.

"Yeah," Frank said. "You can forget the humble act. This is the wrong time to use it."

Moonshadow scowled at him. With a shake of her head, she tossed her crinkly hair back from her face.

"I think when we left the discussion, I was reminding Jackson that the fate of the starship crew is in his hands."

"And Steve Benson's hands," I added. "I have a question. If it's this difficult to convince me, how do you expect to get Steve to cooperate?"

"There's no time for that, now," Moonshadow said, frowning at me. "We'll just have to hope that his real self can remember and play his role accordingly."

"Then you had sure as hell better make sure that I know what I'm supposed to do!"

"We each have our roles," Moonshadow responded, sagely refusing to be baited. "Some of us already know them, but for the benefit of those who don't, I'll review. Starship Falcon Command was composed of twelve officers and a crew of one hundred forty-four thousand."

"One hundred forty-four thousand?" I gasped.

"Remember, Jackson. These beings were to populate the star system they had manifested."

"But only twelve officers for a crew that large?"

"Let me interrupt," Kyanith said. "I know the point Jackson is trying to make. With a crew that large and the few officers, wouldn't the conditions be ideal for insurrection? Am I correct, Jackson?"

"After a fashion."

"That's why I want to answer your question," Kyanith said. "You're thinking of officers in traditional military and government terms—men or women of authority and importance?"

"That's the concept I hold," I admitted. "Is there another?"

"We have no proper word in our language to describe the roles of these twelve," Kyanith continued, "and I know you've been really put off by Moonshadow's authoritative attitude."

"As a matter of fact, I have been. Moonshadow exemplifies my idea of what I consider an officer to be."

"Someone who knows more than you do? Someone who can function better than you can? Someone with more power than you?"

"Yes."

"And who is eager to let you know how much more advanced he or she is," Kyanith continued. "Someone who wants you to know how much more important he is?"

"You've defined what I would call an officer," I said.

"I was afraid of that," Kyanith said, looking at Moonshadow. "I don't mean to take away your glory, Moonshadow, but I think that it's very important right now that Jackson understand this concept."

"Go ahead," Moonshadow said, shrugging.

"These twelve members of the starship that we call officers might better be termed advisors, or teachers, or guides," Kyanith explained. "These beings had no need for authoritarian structure. They felt no desire for a hierarchy. *All members of that starship were equal in authority.* The officers were simply older souls who had accumulated more experience." She paused, looking at me steadily. Then she turned back to the figure in the middle of the circle. "Thank you, Moonshadow."

"Sure," Moonshadow said. She looked down at her hands which lay clasped in her lap. Then she raised her head and stared at me, defiance brightening her blue eyes. Finally, she spoke.

"Each of these twelve officers had functions."

I nodded.

"The commander, Ehkama, had as his function the reuniting of all beings in his charge. Ehkama was, in experiental terms, the oldest of the souls on Starship Falcon Command. His function was termed Unity."

"And?" I prompted.

"This being lived his last life as the man you called Gordon Anderson."

"Papa Gordon?"

Moonshadow nodded.

"I can accept that."

"Good. Now, from here, we go to the second officers. There were two of them, equal in every way, but one hundred eighty degrees apart. Complete opposites. A Twin Soul. These two, Evantar and Etal, came into being at the exact same moment and were, experientally, the second oldest soul on the starship."

"Etal!" I gasped, remembering the nightmare when Susan and I had crossed the creek, years ago, it seemed.

"I see that you have some recall," Moonshadow said, nodding. "The other half of your Twin Soul, Evantar, you know as Steve Benson."

I stifled the snort I wanted to sound. If Papa Gordon's purpose had been reuniting souls and his title was Unity, I hesitated to think of the title that Moonshadow would confer on Steve and me, considering our purpose was rescuing souls.

"The other nine beings were, experientally, the third oldest of the souls," Moonshadow said. "I was one of those souls. My name is Eltera and my function was as Record Keeper. The one you call Kyanith is Esami. Esami is a Sensitive and you have had direct experience with her function. Ekalia and Ertouk, or Elizabeth Anderson and Jason Cartwright, were a Twin Soul whose purpose was creating circumstances to allow soul growth.

"Ephera's purpose is to stimulate views into probable lives and realities. She is called Susan and her function is Awakener. The Historian, who works closely with the Record Keeper, is Edmir, the one we call Frank. Enakor, the one known as Dorrie, has, as her purpose, the stimulation of creativity. She is the Inspiror. The last of the group, our

Communicator, Eshata, is responsible for keeping Falcon Command in contact with the Mother Ship. You know Eshata as Marvin Garland."

I breathed a sigh of relief. All of this really hadn't been necessary for my sake. Some of the information could have stimulated notes for a novel, but I wasn't sure I would ever use it. Then, a question arose in my mind.

"What about the twelfth officer? You only described eleven."

"So you *were* listening," Moonshadow said. "The last officer, Emara, had, as his purpose, the balancing of polarities. He was the Magnetizer."

"Then, get him to dissolve that force field!" I demanded. "He's the expert!"

I stopped speaking. Each person in the group had focused his stare on me. I had the feeling that I had seriously breached starship etiquette.

"What's wrong?" I asked. "Did I say something wrong?"

"Emara was working on the force field when the shift occurred," Susan said.

"The rest of us were in the air," Kyanith added. "We were locked outside the tunnel and the one hundred forty-four thousand members of the crew were locked inside the tunnel."

"Emara was between worlds," Moonshadow explained. "He had time to manifest his storage cubicle, but not enough time to get past the force field and inside the tunnel. Emara is lost."

Chapter Twenty-Five

More than the worst movie I'd ever seen, the most terrible book I'd ever read, this story kept going from bad to worse to worst. Each time, I had taken a deep breath, telling myself that, regardless of how ridiculous and unbelievable the concept, I would make an attempt to accept it. And, each time, the next information released was even more difficult to comprehend.

"Storage cubicles?" I ventured. "Like coffins?"

"Similar," Moonshadow said. "The cubicles are a hybrid mixture of hospital bed and coffin. The starship crew is in a state that is called, in your terms, suspended animation. They await our rescue. Then they will awaken and continue their purposes."

I shook my head and bit my tongue. I would offer no rebuttal to this revelation.

"What about Emara?" Susan asked. "Will we be able to revitalize him when the time arrives?"

"Only if we can return the cubicle to the tunnel entrance before the force field is dissolved," Moonshadow said.

"You *know* where he is?" I asked.

"I have the storage cubicle," Kyanith said. "It's in my room upstairs, in the loft."

Nausea compounded the piercing pain in my temples. My vision blurred as I watched Kyanith run up the steps and into the cabin. I am Jackson Cody, I told myself. I know who I am and I know that this is a dream. It has to be. Why, though, couldn't I awaken? I raised my head and looked at Moonshadow, her Victorian pose incongruous with her flower child dress. I'm really much more creative than I had realized, I told myself, as my eyes circled the group and came to rest on Frank. In my most surrealistic of plots, I would never have cast my brother as a homosexual. The absurdity of a fifteen year old girl keeping a dead alien, coffin-bound, in her bedroom provided comedy relief to the farce. My thoughts must have surfaced and changed the expression on my face because Susan spoke.

"What's so funny, Jackson? Share it. We can use some cheer."

"Nothing," I said, shrugging my shoulders. I smiled at her and remembered what Mama Kate had told me so long ago about my nightmares. "*Know that you created them,*" she had said. "*Your dreams are populated with people and events that you have thought of and about. You are in charge. Only you can decide where your dream is to go.*"

"She was right," I whispered.

"What?"

I looked at Susan and frowned. I felt a wave of irritation travel over my body. I needed to make her stronger, I thought, disliking the underlying whine in her question. Yes, Susan should be as independent and confident as she had been in our youth.

"My guides tell me he is weakening," Moonshadow intoned, inclining her head toward me. "And our time is perilously short."

I intensely disliked Moonshadow's patronage. And her air of superiority. I would transform her into what she thought she was—a calm, peaceful, non-critical saint. I watched her turn to Frank and open her mouth. When no words came out, the puzzled look on her face was reward enough for me.

I hadn't liked Frank since he was about eight years old. And I didn't care for the man he was in this dream. So, the present Frank had to go. I remembered the Frank-child of yore, uninhibited, gleeful, practical, and decisive. This was my dream and I was in charge. Frank's psyche would be that of my long-ago brother.

I breathed deeply and scooted my back against the rough bark of the elm. Deciding to change the anxiety-producing course of this dream had been a true inspiration. I hadn't felt this good in years. No, I corrected myself, I hadn't felt this good since the present dream had started.

Hearing the cabin door open, I looked toward the porch to see Kyanith. She carried a large, rectangular shaped bundle, wrapped in a red and black striped blanket. Moonshadow struggled to her feet and rushed toward the girl.

"I'll help you, Kyanith," she said softly, lifting the burden from the girl's arms. Kyanith, surprised, stood still and Moonshadow walked back to the circle. Instead of returning to the grassy central position she'd occupied earlier, Moonshadow laid the bundle on the ground between Frank and the tree that Susan and I leaned against. Gently, she began rolling off the woolen wrapping.

"Papa Gordon found it almost forty years ago," Frank spoke. "It was lying near the spot where we believe Elmer Cody to have disappeared. Somewhere, deep inside, Papa Gordon knew what it was and he saved it. It's been locked in his safe at Gordon's Glen all of these years."

Down to the last layer of bundling, Moonshadow slowly pulled the cover off. Lying in the folds of the blanket, sparkling dully in the sunlight, lay a crystal collector's dream. I stood up and walked over to study the large, clear tabulator crystal. It was approximately two feet long, eight inches wide, and half that thick. Seventeen smoky blue chevrons, perfectly spaced, colored the length of the crystal. Mama Kate's voice came to me across a great distance: *You are in charge.*

*   *   *

It would take some growing accustomed to, I thought, watching the four heads bend reverently over the crystal. A few things might still surprise me, but I had created this situation and, as in my novels and short stories, it must have a logical and timely ending. The tunnel must be opened. Inside it, lay one hundred forty four thousand more of these grisly coffins and they must be recovered.

"Where do we go from here?" I asked. "Do we need to carry Emara to the tunnel? How are we going to get him inside, past the force field?"

Susan stared at me and frowned. Moonshadow looked puzzled and Frank appeared shocked. Kyanith, however, smiled at me.

"Good thinking," she said, her face happy. I told myself that I would work on blunting her sensitivity. A fifteen year old shouldn't have to take on all of the heavy emotions and responsibilities that Kyanith had been burdened with.

"We shall go to the tunnel immediately after we review polarities," Moonshadow said, standing up and facing me. Her face wore a placid, bovine expression. Good God, I thought, it's really working. She's beginning to live her new role. Glancing at Frank, I saw him busily wrapping the bundle back, directing Susan and Kyanith as to how to fold corners. He said something and the two women laughed. I marveled at my creativity. Why hadn't I thought of this earlier? I wanted to ask one of them about Steve Benson, but I decided against it. If he had to come into my dream, I would think about it then, and not before.

"How are we going to get Emara through the force field?" I persisted.

147

"We'll find a way," Frank said, looking up from the last fold on the bundle. "I don't think we have anything to worry about."

"Compared to what we've already done," Susan said, standing up and turning to me, "this should be no trouble."

What had I done? Their confidence, virulently contagious, infected me and I knew that I could do whatever needed to be done. I found myself enjoying the dream.

Chapter Twenty-Six

"Do you think that they'll be okay?" I asked Susan. Five minutes earlier, Kyanith, Moonshadow, and Frank had taken off up the trail to the mine. Kyanith and Moonshadow carried the blanketed crystal and Frank led the way.

"Sure," she said. "There's nothing to fret about, especially now that you understand about polarities and how you are to fulfill your function."

"Let's go over it again," I suggested. "I want to make sure I'm right. We have only one emotion. Right?"

Susan nodded.

"Everything that we feel is a variation of that one emotion?"

"Yes," she agreed.

"Love, for instance, can fall anywhere on the emotional spectrum, from the positive to the negative. When it is possessive, it is bad, and when..."

"Jackson!" Susan cried. "Stop!"

"Why?"

"Don't use good and bad! The polarities of emotion are positive and negative!"

"I forgot," I apologized. "I'm so accustomed to thinking of bad and negative as synonymous. And the same for good and positive."

"Throw away the concept of good and bad," Susan pleaded. "Think of emotion as a see-saw, with positive on one end and negative on the other. You want the board perfectly level. You must have the same weight on both ends."

"No other way?"

"You must have some other possibility in mind or you wouldn't have asked."

"What about different weights placed at varying distances from the end of the board?" I asked. "A larger weight on one end could be moved closer to the center. That would also create balance."

"Good thought."

"Or, the board could be longer on one end," I suggested.

"Okay, okay," Susan laughed. "Just so long as you realize that balance is the key."

"That brings me to another question. Liz and Jason were perfectly balanced. Their emotions were identical. What happened?"

"Liz and Jason *were* perfectly balanced," Susan agreed. "But they were balanced exactly the same."

"That sounds ideal."

"It *is* ideal," Susan said. "It's ideal for a Twin Soul. Liz had forgotten, however, that they were balanced as a unit."

"I don't get the point."

Susan sighed. She shook her bangs back from her forehead and looked into the distance, toward the trail leading to the mine. Then she spoke.

"Imagine the see-saw again. Think of one end as Positive Ten and the other end as Negative Ten. The middle is Zero. Assume that all degrees of emotion fall between Positive Ten and Negative Ten."

"I'm with you."

"Take one of your everyday feelings. Frustration, for instance. It can make you feel powerless, or it can spur you to action."

"So, frustration can be both positive and negative."

"Yes," Susan said. Then she paused, clasping her hands together and frowning.

"Go on. I'm listening."

"I'm simplifying this almost to the point of inaccuracy," she said. "Let's say that Positive Frustration is a Plus Three and Negative Frustration is a Minus Three."

"They're balanced."

"Now, add anger," Susan suggested. "You feel anger because you think that someone or something has taken away some of your strength. That is the negative end. Again, as a positive, anger can force you to move."

"I see."

"Now, give Positive Anger a Plus Three and Negative Anger a Minus Three. Combining the two aspects of emotion, frustration and anger, what do you have?"

"A Minus Five and a Plus Five," I said. "A perfect balance."

"Correct," Susan agreed, still frowning. "This explanation is so artificial using only two variations of emotion."

"I'll take that into consideration. Just continue."

"Okay. Take frustration again. This time, let it be worth Minus Two on the Negative end and Plus Three on the Positive end."

"It's unbalanced."

"But, add negative anger worth Minus Three and positive anger worth Plus Two. Now, what is the score?"

"A Minus Five and a Plus Five," I said, feeling almost dizzy with the enlightened thought. "Between the two feelings and their respective values, you have balanced emotion!"

"Can you carry it on out, Jackson? Can you see what could happen when you add in all of the possible degrees of emotion owned by two beings?"

"I think I'm beginning to understand," I said, grasping for the thought. "Even though the beings are perfectly balanced with each other, the separate variations of emotion are not."

Susan remained silent.

"I finally see your point," I continued. "Liz and Jason were balanced as a *total*. And you're saying that Steve and I have to balance, not only on total emotion, but on every variation?"

"You always have," Susan said. "This is not a new concept. But, every time that you've been called upon to use this balance, one or the other of you has shifted position on some vital feeling."

"We've tried this before?"

"Many times."

"Why can't I remember? If this is so godawful important, I should have some recollection!"

"When the time is right, you'll remember."

"You'll have to do better than that, Susan. If I don't know how I failed previously, how will I know how to avoid the same pitfall the next time?"

"I don't know if I can explain," Susan said. "You and Steve are the only beings who fully understand."

"Damn!" I shouted, forgetting, for a moment, that it was my dream.

"Marvin was with you the last time you made the attempt," Susan began. "You, Steve, and Marvin were three gold miners here in Arkansas in the middle part of the nineteenth century."

"We were the three who disappeared?"

"Yes. As I understand it, events were proceeding as they should

151

until you began to feel guilt about Steve's pain. The guilt dropped all the way into the extreme negative end and the polarities became unbalanced."

"What happened to us? To our physical bodies?"

"You dematerialized the bodies, de-briefed yourselves, and came back as three other physical beings."

"And failed again, I suppose."

"No. That was the last attempt. Until now."

"Why is it so urgent now?"

Susan sighed again. She stood up and moved away. I watched her profile when she opened her mouth, as if to speak. Then she closed it and turned to look at me. After a long silence, she spoke.

"Since the mishap, there have been only six periods of two hundred years each in which the planets of this star system have been aligned correctly for this rescue to occur."

"You're kidding me! I thought the only alignment we had to worry about was between Steve and me!"

"No," Susan said, shaking her head. "The planetary alignment occurs only for one short period every twenty-six thousand years. And, it is correct for only one twenty-four hour period every fifty years of that two hundred."

"And, I take it, we must be entering the last year of that two hundred year cycle."

"This is Year One Hundred Fifty," Susan said. "But, remember the other factors that have to be considered. The first year of the cycle, Year Zero, you failed. That was the abortive attempt we discussed earlier. At Year Fifty, you had not chosen to be on this planet. At Year One Hundred, you and Steve were friends and weren't balanced correctly."

"And this twenty-four hour period," I asked. "When does it begin?"

"It began at midnight," Susan said, holding up her wrist and looking at her watch. "We have only twelve hours left."

Chapter Twenty-Seven

I want a normal friend, I thought, squeezing my eyes closed, wishing for Simon Feathers and the heady gasoline smell of the service station in Albuquerque. I want a normal conversation about who is selling dope at the parking lot of the truck stop and about which lady pulled up her skirt to offer Simon her goods. Instead, I'm stuck here in this forgotten dream. There's no place to go except to the Violet Fern. And there's nothing else to do other than shatter that damned force field.

When I opened my eyes, Susan had gone. I looked up the hill, searching through the palm trees for the path. *Palm trees?* Shit, I had drifted off into another dream. Palms don't grow in Arkansas! And the sunlight! It was softer, more diffused, almost as if there were a giant filter between earth and the golden orb. The air, though humid, cloaked my body in comfort. This dream was much more pleasant than the last one. I leaned back against the tree, planning to enjoy this.

"Where is the masterpiece?"

The deep, thunderous voice pulled me to an upright position and I struggled to my feet, looking around for the source.

"Look within," came the voice again. Although the nuances and tones were familiar, I couldn't recognize the speaker.

"Where are you?" I yelled. The palms absorbed my voice and a pristine stillness surrounded me. "I can't see you."

"You were to study the probability," the voice continued, ignoring my questions. The tones echoed in my head, vibrating my skull.

Study the probability? How could a probability be examined? The very word itself denoted that an event *might* occur. Was I reduced to dissecting might-have-beens?

"Who *are* you?" I demanded of the omnipresent voice. "Do I know you?"

"Better than you know yourself," the voice, hollow and distant now, toned.

"Don't go," I cried, turning around and looking for the source of the message. "What is a probability?"

The air, comfortable only seconds earlier, pressed in on me, heavy and ominous. My lungs labored and I gasped for breath. Strong hands gripped my shoulders.

"Jackson! Take it easy. Relax and you won't have so much trouble breathing!"

My eyes traveled over the denim clad legs and up to the white face.

"Help!" I gasped. "Can't breathe. Susan, help!"

My head lolled forward as I felt her shake my shoulders. My lungs constricted and I fought the black dots in front of my eyes.

"You're hyperventilating, Jackson. Here, breathe with me."

She held my face tightly against her chest. As I listened to the hypnotic beat of her heart, my breath came more easily.

"That's better," she said gently. She released my head. "What did you do to cause that?"

As I told her of the dream, the vision, the hallucination, I watched relief spread over the tight skin of her face. When I reached the point about probabilities, she smiled.

"What *is* a probability?" I asked, chagrined. "Earlier, Moonshadow mentioned that you were in charge of that area."

Susan nodded.

"Well, tell me," I demanded. "You've got me to this point, you might as well finish me off."

"For every action, thought, or emotion that comes into being," Susan said, "there are dozens, no hundreds, of other ways in which that action, thought, or emotion might be expressed. For every word that you speak, you have searched through your stored memory for the exact expression you use."

"That would require some awfully fast thinking."

"When you consider that this entire lifetime is just as a blink of the eye, then time loses importance."

I nodded, forcing myself to remember that this whole thing was a dream. That, in fact, it wouldn't last more than a few seconds. Thought of that way, Susan's proposition made sense.

"For every decision you've made," she continued, "There are many other options you could have chosen."

"Right," I said, remembering my decision to play along with this dream.

"Take an example," she said. "Suppose that, in your travels, you came to a crossroad. You decided to go to the right. But, there were other choices."

"I could have gone left," I said. "Or, straight ahead."

"You could have turned around and gone back the way you came," she added, "or, you could have stayed in the one spot."

"Okay," I said. "But, what difference does it make? None of those possibilities is important. I eliminated them by making the decision to go right."

"Did you?"

"Sure, I did. Listen, Susan, are you implying that I could have taken more than one of those roads? Look, I'm only one person!"

"When you're really involved in the decision-making process," Susan said, "it sometimes becomes difficult, almost impossible, to turn loose of the other possibilities."

I thought of my decision to marry Chris Vining. Up to that point, a large part of my soul had retained the dream that Susan would call me and the two of us would be reunited. My decision to marry Chris had eliminated that possibility.

"Wait, Susan. Even when I've made a decision to do one thing, I can still go back and do the other?"

"You don't have to go back."

"What?"

"When you're truly ego-involved, pardon the expression, you can't make a decision."

"What do I do? Just twiddle my thumbs?"

"You're confronted with three actions that could occur—very probably *might* occur. You can go forward, you can go back; you can choose not to move. Eventually, you make a decision, even if it is the simple choice *not* to make a decision. Because of your 'ego-involvement,' a fragment of your personality breaks off and carries through with the other choice, or choices."

"That kind of thinking is schizophrenic!"

"Perhaps."

"Well, can you think of a better way to describe what you've just told me?"

"Jackson, you asked me to explain probabilities and I'm trying. What you do with the information, if anything, is up to you."

"Well, I'm not carrying this discussion back to reality," I mumbled.

"What?"

"Nothing. Go on with this alter-ego bit."

"Alter-ego is not the term I'd choose," Susan said, frowning at me. "Although, from your point of view, I suppose it's understandable that you think in terms of novel structure. And, that may be as good a way as any for you to comprehend."

I found myself growing impatient with this roundabout, hazy explanation. I tried to remember any other discussion I'd had in which a strange concept had been introduced and I'd had such difficulty accepting it. In college, Dr. Hathaway, my advisor, and I had generated many a heated debate over atheism. But, a little voice niggled at me, even atheism was based on the denial of a concept I'd already accepted. This alien concept of probabilities dumfounded me. Time and space didn't exist: there was no good, no bad. I wasn't even sure that I existed.

"Then explain to me, Susan," I said, frustration sharpening my voice. "I'm here in Arkansas. Is there a little piece of me in Albuquerque, pumping gas?"

"You could say that," she agreed. "A decision was necessary in order for you to come back here. Because of memories and insecurities, it would have been easier for you to remain in Albuquerque. You chose, however, to come here."

"You're right. I struggled with that decision. I spent hours going over the pros and cons."

"You created dozens of scenarios," Susan said. "You acted out roles in each of these vignettes."

"I did a lot of daydreaming," I said. "I thought about coming here, of staying there, of running away somewhere where my agent couldn't find me. I even thought about pretending that the message hadn't reached me."

"With each daydream," Susan interrupted. "You sent out a fragment of yourself to, in a sense, test the experience."

"Like my dream characters!" I exclaimed. Then I stopped. "But that means…"

"Yes," Susan said. "Each of those fragments is continuing with that existence you created for him."

"That's crazy! I considered going to New Orleans. Are you saying that there is a fragment of me in New Orleans right now?"

"Stop and think about it, Jackson. You created the probable you. He had all of your memories and experiences. You also created a probable situation for him. Yes, he exists in that probability at this very moment. If your decision had been to go to New Orleans, then *this* Jackson, the one here with me, would have been a probability."

"Perhaps I am," I whispered, thinking of the dreamlike state of the past few hours. "How can I distinguish the real me from a probable me?"

"Does it matter?" Susan asked. "All realities—probable, dream, or this one—contribute experience to our growth. Your probable Jackson in New Orleans thinks that *he* is the real Jackson."

"Hold on," I said. "This probable me in New Orleans, or the one in Albuquerque—I can learn from *his* experiences?"

"Jackson," Susan said, walking over to me and placing her hand on my forearm. "As an entity, you are so much greater than this physical body that you call yourself. You, above all others, should grasp that! As a writer, you have called it creativity, or inspiration. But you have drawn constantly from that higher source, that combination of all *yous*."

"I'll accept it, Susan. But I'm not sure that I understand. And, I certainly don't agree."

"You don't have to understand, or agree. You don't even have to accept. The growth will occur, whether or not you try."

"Then, what the hell am I doing here?"

"This is the reality you chose to experience."

"Damn it, Susan. I didn't count on this."

"You knew," she said. "You even know the end of the story. That's why you chose this probability."

It's a dream, I consoled myself. And there's a dream within the dream. And, on and on to the point of dizziness. I thought about the earlier dream with a young Susan and a baby Kyanith.

"I wonder what would have happened if I hadn't married Chris," I ventured. "I wonder what would have happened if I had, instead, come back here to you."

"I'm sure you already know."

"I think I glimpsed that probability last night," I said, "after we brought Kyanith to the cabin."

"Oh?"

"Yes. The probable me had come here to the cabin. Papa Gordon had helped you to remodel it and you and Kyanith were living here. Kyanith was just an infant. I think I had just found out about her and had only a short time here before I had to rush back somewhere."

"I have my own probabilities about that event," Susan admitted. "Where had you been?"

"I think I must have been on military leave," I said, remembering the blue uniform. "That's right. I was due to leave for Vietnam within the week."

157

How did I know this? Some of it hadn't even been a part of that dream. Puzzled, I stared at Susan.

"This is weird," I said. "All of those years ago, when I didn't hear from you, I did a lot of thinking about enlisting in the air force. Even stranger, I can't remember why I chose, instead, to marry Chris."

"You knew how that probability would end," Susan said, kneeling down beside me.

"I do," I said, surprised. "I was in Vietnam only weeks before my plane was shot down. Good God, I was killed!"

"There's the reason that you didn't follow that probability, Jackson. Somewhere inside you, you remembered this mission and, because of that, chose to do as you did."

Chapter Twenty-Eight

"So, there are probable *mes* and probable *yous* and probable *events*."

"There are even probable *lives* and probable *universes*," Susan said. She had dropped to the ground and stretched out, resting her head on my thigh. She again looked at her wristwatch.

"I'm giving them twenty more minutes," she said. "If they're not back by then, we'll go to the Violet Fern."

"Suits me," I said. "I'm ready to get on with this."

I felt Susan's head nod against my knee. She closed her eyes and I felt tender concern flow through my veins. Susan hadn't slept anymore than I in the last thirty hours or so; she must be exhausted. But I needed answers to other questions.

"Susan?" Her eyelids fluttered and she opened her eyes. "Susan, right before I had trouble breathing, I could have visited a probable reality. The dream or vision I mentioned?"

"Tell me about it," she said. She closed her eyes, but I knew that I had her attention.

"I was in a place almost like this," I began. "Instead of pines and oaks, palm trees were scattered around the landscape. The vegetation was tropical. And the air, too," I said, remembering the drapery of humid air around my shoulders. "There seemed to be a thick cloud between me and the sun. It was pleasant until I began having trouble breathing. The air was so thick that I couldn't seem to breathe enough oxygen. It was like a locked steam room."

"You did visit a probable universe," Susan said, opening her eyes and sitting up. "When the beings first manifested this star system, they thought of several other universes and star systems. Because they had been created in thought, these other universes continued to exist. Apparently, there had been little damaging activity on your probable

159

planet to destroy the hydrosphere."

"Hydrosphere? Did you mean atmosphere? Ionosphere?"

"No," she said. "On your probable planet, the seas had not yet descended. The water remained as a three-mile thick protective coating for the planet's surface, shielding its inhabitants from the damaging rays of the sun. Did you see any of the people? Did you look at your own body?"

"I didn't see anyone." I said. "But a powerful voice came to me, seemingly from all around, chastising me about losing the master-pieces. It said I was supposed to study the probability."

"The inhabitants of that planet had most likely never manifested physical bodies," Susan said. "They had no way to experience the dynamics of physical relationships, especially the group dynamics of this struggle here at the Violet Fern. The voice was telling a probable you on a probable planet that you were to observe and learn from this experience."

"But, the voice called this situation the probability."

"Certainly. Remember that we said the probable you in New Orleans thought *he* was the real Jackson?"

"I see. So the probable me on that probable planet thought he was the real me?"

"Or *you* think that you are the real you."

* * *

This discussion could drive a person crazy, I thought, comprehending, for the first time, the full meaning of the phrase. I touched Susan's shoulder.

"What time is it?" I asked. "They're not back."

"We ought to go," Susan said, rising to her feet. She held a hand to me and I grabbed it, feeling the stiffness in my body as I stood.

"You lead," I said, gently shoving her ahead of me. As she started the climb, she looked back over her shoulder at me.

"Do you think you're ready for this?" she asked.

"I'm ready," I told her. "You would be better off worrying about Steve."

She headed up the path, climbing briskly, but surely. Halfway to the top, she turned again to look at me. Concern reflected from her features.

"Sit down and rest, Jackson," she ordered, coming back toward me. "Sit on that rock beside the trail. Right there on your left."

Relieved, I found the flat rock and dropped to it. Liquid glued my shirt to my back and I felt streams of perspiration course down my neck.

160

It had been much easier this morning, climbing up the trail after my pique with Moonshadow.

"Here," Susan said, pulling a white handkerchief from her shirt pocket. "Let me wipe your face."

I felt her gentle hands pat the moisture from my forehead and cheeks. I took the cloth from her hand and ran it around my neck.

"I feel more like eighty than forty," I said, handing the handkerchief back to Susan. She dropped her eyes as she took the sweaty rag from my outstretched hand.

"Just rest, Jackson. We'll try again, shortly."

"Speaking of feeling eighty," I said. "I had forgotten about another probable me. It was different, though."

"How's that?"

"Well, according to my conception of probabilities, I sort of flip into the probable body of my probable self and experience the event the way he would have."

"That's one probability," Susan said, smiling.

"Well, I met a real, flesh-and-blood me," I stated, squinting my eyes to observe her expression. "He was much older, but he was me. He was close enough for me to touch and we talked."

"What did you discuss?"

"We talked about a camping trip in Canada six years ago," I said. "Well, to me it was six years ago. He said it happened twenty years ago."

"There's your time factor again," Susan said. "Shot to hell."

"Yeah."

Susan busied herself tying a loose lace on one of her shoes. I looked off toward the valley. The cabin's metal roof glinted in the sunlight.

"We were one person until that day that I saw the rainbow," I mused. "I can recall wondering what it felt like to walk through a rainbow. But, I didn't. I stayed at the campsite."

"And *he* walked through the rainbow."

"He just went on with life from that point," I said. "He forgot me completely. And I'm the one who gave him life."

"Are you sure about that?" Susan asked, looking into my eyes. "Are you positive that the probable you was the one who left? Couldn't the probable you have been the one who stayed?"

"God, Susan, you provoke the most intellect-draining possibilities. If I am a probable me, then none of this is necessary. I'm not real."

"Do you believe that?"

"I don't know, Susan. Anymore, I have no conception of reality. I keep bouncing in and out of hallucinations, or probable realities, as you call them. I think I'm real until I come back here, to this," I said, emphasizing my point by slapping my knee. "This is what I call the *real* me. But, somehow or another. I can't let go of those others."

"Why do you feel that you need to let them go?"

"Because they're not *real*!"

Susan laughed. She rubbed at a scratch on her boot. When she looked up at me, her eyes still held mirth.

"Tell me why you keep insisting that this is the only reality," she said.

"Because I'm *here*," I shouted. "There's only one thing I'm sure about anymore. *I am*! *I exist*! I am…"

I stopped, feeling my words trail off before they reached my vocal cords. I swallowed, feeling saliva push past the lump made by my unspoken words.

"Don't you feel the same way in your other realities?"

"No," I said. "Last night, when I stumbled at the creek and fell, I flipped into another probable life. It was similar to this one, except that you and Mama Kate were two people named Miranda, my wife, and Katie, an Indian medicine woman."

"Who were you?"

"I was Jackson," I said. "I kept trying to tell you and Mama Kate who I was. Both of you kept calling me Campbell, insisting that I was someone else."

"Anything else?"

"Yes," I said. "It happened at another time."

"In the past?"

"No."

"The future, then."

"No," I said. "It was as if the time were now. The people, however, had developed nuclear and solar energy rather than relying on hydro-electric power. We were in a small house made of some type of glass that lit up. There were no light bulbs."

"A probable reality?"

"It certainly wasn't *this* one," I said. "They weren't even interested in the Violet Fern!" I paused for a moment. "But, they *knew* about it. They didn't call it the Violet Fern, just mentioned it as a possible source for crystals to be used in their solar collectors."

"Gordon Anderson named the Violet Fern almost fifty years ago," Susan said. "So your probability split occurred before he named it.

Otherwise, they would have known it as such."

"They knew something about the crystals and the force field," I said. "The one named Katie called me Etal and she knew that you—Miranda, that is—and I had been talking about the mine."

Susan looked at me. She nodded, gesturing that I continue.

"She wanted to keep me in that world," I said. "When she realized that she wouldn't be able to do so, she told me to talk to Kyanith."

"So this Katie had some awareness of your present reality and also about the Violet Fern. It seems that she knew you in that reality and in this one, too."

"Katie had the same powers as Kyanith," I exclaimed. "She removed my confusion and fears by touching my temples."

"Your fears? Or Campbell's fears?"

"You were pregnant," I said, ignoring her question. "I think that you had miscarried twice before. We were concerned that the same thing might happen again."

I hesitated. Events and experiences flooded back.

"It was Sarah's and Papa Gordon's probability," I said, amazed at the insight. "In this life, the one right here, Sarah married Elmer and Papa Gordon married Mama Kate. In that probability, Sarah married Papa Gordon. That's when it started."

"Go on."

"Frank and I were named Stuart and Campbell. Mama Kate never married. You and Marvin were brother and sister. After college, Frank went to Scotland to teach philosophy and I married you. We built a home down the river, south of Gordon's Glen, and I wrote mysteries. I became quite famous and we were well-to-do."

"Nice change," Susan said drily.

"In that life," I continued, "there were no wars after World War One. The uranium that contributed to the atomic bomb in this reality was developed, instead, as an alternative energy source in that reality.'"

"There was no conflict?" Susan asked. "We know that the need for recovering the starship must also have existed in that life. Where was Steve? Who was he?"

"Steve was the unborn child you carried," I said, amazed at the revelation. "He would have been my son!"

"Your son? Or Campbell's son?"

I didn't have the opportunity to answer. The loud sound of an unmuffled engine came from a distance to our left, toward the road up to the mine. Shortly after the sound reached my ears, a horn began honking at steady, regular intervals. Susan jumped to her feet and I followed suit.

"That's Marvin's pickup," Susan said, grabbing my hand. "I'd recognize that horn anywhere!"

Chapter Twenty-Nine

My legs denied their previous lethargy and I followed Susan up the steep shortcut to the parking area above the open pit. She had been correct. Parked in the middle of the clearing, engine still ticking, Marvin's pickup painted a yellow splash against the torn red earth of the landslide. The door on the driver's side was open and my eyes scoured the immediate area, searching for my friend. Then I heard the scream from below. Susan and I stared at each other before breaking into a run toward the sound.

Although I had recognized the cry of anguish as female I was not prepared for the sight that awaited my eyes when I reached the halfway point on the carved stone stairs and the tunnel opening came into view. Down below, Frank and Moonshadow stood on either side of a prone female. Kyanith knelt beside the girl, using her shirttail to wipe blood from the ravaged face. I stopped dead and Susan's weight pushed into me from the rear. For a moment, we tottered on the hillside before I regained my balance.

"What the hell?" I gasped.

"It's Dorrie," Susan cried. "Dorrie Jacobs. She works at Steve's motel."

"I know who she is," I said, grabbing Susan's hand and pulling her on down the steps. "But, what is she doing here? Where is Marvin?"

At that moment, Frank looked up and, seeing us, a relieved smile passed over his face. He limped toward us.

"Frank," Susan cried, slipping around me and running down the last few steps. "What has happened to Dorrie?"

Frank shrugged. Over Susan's head, his eyes bore into mine.

"Where's Marvin?" I asked. "That's his pickup up there."

"You'll have to ask Dorrie," he said, turning his back and following Susan.

165

Dorrie screamed again and Kyanith laid her head on the girl's chest, hugging her tightly. The scream faded and Dorrie began crying softly. I was close enough now to see the ugly cuts and dark bruises on her face, to recognize the particular crooked angle of a broken arm. Had she driven the pickup all the way from Bethel Bluff?

Susan bent down beside Kyanith and pulled her daughter off Dorrie's chest. An electric look passed between the two before Susan reached for Dorrie's good hand, taking it in her own and cradling it gently.

"Dorrie, can you hear me?" she asked softly.

In contrast to the bruised flesh surrounding them, Dorrie's violet eyes seemed unnaturally large when she opened them. Responding to the strength behind Susan's question, she spoke.

"It was Steve," she whispered. I moved closer. "He beat me up. He was going to kill me."

I watched tears edge out of the corners of her eyes, following tiny wrinkles out toward her ears. With her free hand, Susan caressed Dorrie's arm, making low, comforting noises.

"You're going to be safe now," she told Dorrie. "I won't let Steve do any more harm to you."

"You can't stop him," she cried. "When Sheriff Garland tried..."

Her voice broke and sobs erupted from her throat. Her body trembled and she rolled over to her side, drawing her knees toward her chest.

"What happened to Marvin?" I demanded sharply, ignoring Susan's glare. "*What has happened to Marvin?*"

I moved past Frank and hunkered down beside Dorrie. Her sobs continued. I put my right hand on her shoulder and silently cursed my move when I felt her shudder.

"I'm sorry," she whimpered. "Sheriff Garland was a good man. He..."

"*Was* a good man?" I yelled, feeling my fingers press into the soft flesh between the fragile bones of Dorrie's shoulder. "What do you *mean?*"

"Stop it, Jackson," Susan ordered, pulling my hand back. "You're only frightening her more."

"He tried to help me," Dorrie whispered. I leaned over in order to better hear her low words. "He gave me his keys and told me to come for you."

Ragged breath escaped my lungs. Marvin hadn't been caught by

166

surprise. He knew what he was up against and I'd bet my life that he could handle Steve Benson.

"Where is he, Dorrie? Where's Marvin?"

"At the motel," she sighed. "I think that he's dead. Steve stabbed him with a big knife."

* * *

The fourteen mile ride into town took a thousand years, each one filled with an odd combination of fear, guilt and anticipation. I was afraid that Dorrie might have been correct, that Marvin may already have been dead. I felt guilt that I hadn't been there to prevent it. The setting sun glinted on brightly painted metal and I pressed the brake pedal on Marvin's pickup, slowing the vehicle to a crawl as I met the semi-truck on the narrow bridge. Hearing the uneven breathing beside me, I remembered, seemingly for the first time since leaving the mine, that Susan sat beside me.

"You still feel I should have stayed there?" I asked her. "Marvin is the best friend I ever had."

Susan remained silent. Out of the corner of my eye, I observed her stiff posture, the rigid clasp of her hands in her lap.

"I have to try and help him," I persisted. "He would have done the same for me!"

Still, she said nothing. Up ahead, on the horizon, I watched the blurred red letters of the Benson's Inn sign come into focus and felt something akin to hatred flow bitterly through my body when I read the words.

"Do you think he's here?" I asked Susan, as we turned into the graveled parking area.

"Your guess is as good as mine," she said. "I sincerely hope so. We only have a few hours left."

"Damn the time," I shouted, slamming on the brakes. Gravel popped on the underside of the pickup. "I happen to think that saving my friend's life is more important than playing out a part in some stupid little supernatural scenario!"

"You're the only one who can make that decision," Susan said, opening her door.

I turned off the ignition, pulled the key out and opened my own door. As an afterthought, I pushed in the light switch and an empty dusk fell around us. I knew something was wrong, but I couldn't put my finger on it until Susan spoke.

"He's here, Jackson. He's turned all the lights off."

I looked at the long. low building in front of us. Reflections from the setting sun and light from the Lamplighter Restaurant next door shone eerily on the cream-colored brick. I felt the skin of my scalp prickle. Steve Benson was in one of those rooms, waiting for me, and he had the strategic advantage. He could see us and know our moves as soon as we made them.

"You stay here, Susan. I'm going in."

"Not by yourself, you're not," she said. "I might, at least, be able to talk to him. You know that you don't have a chance. He won't listen to a word you say."

"Have it your way," I said. Could it have been only a few hours earlier that I had been so caught up in the mass hysteria at the Violet Fern? Or, was *this* a dream? I headed toward the office, feeling the gravel crunch underneath my hiking boots. There was no sound from within and I turned the knob, flinging the door inward and stepping to the side. Silence greeted me.

"He's not in here," Susan said. "Let me get a light turned on."

I felt her brush past me and heard the click as she turned the switch. She sighed.

"He's shut off the electricity," she said. "I know where the circuit box is located. Just wait here."

Seconds ticked off into endless minutes. I heard the crunch of Susan's feet on the gravel, heard the hollow sound of the circuit box being opened and the grinding sound of the switch being pulled. Then the lights were working again and my eyes darted around the room before coming to rest on a bloody object on the desk in front of me.

"God," I moaned, trying to move my gaze. I felt Susan's warmth return to my side, felt her body stiffen as she looked at the desk. The backs of my knees grew weak and I sat down on a nearby chair, feeling the air escape through the seams of the naugahyde upholstery. Susan moved closer to the desk.

"It's a finger," she gasped. Then she turned to me, green eyes wide. "Jackson, Steve cut off Marvin's finger!"

"I know," I said. My words came through a hollow tunnel. Somewhere in the background of buzzing noises in my ears, I heard a familiar sound. An engine started. A car pulled out of the parking area, throwing gravel on the surrounding vehicles.

"That's Steve," Susan cried, running to the door. I jumped up beside her, watching the rapidly disappearing taillights. "I think there's someone in the car with him. Was it Marvin?"

"It could have been," I answered. My tongue felt thick. "I want to check the rooms here. Make sure."

"There's a master key over there," Susan said, moving around the desk, carefully averting her eyes from the desktop. She grabbed a large keyring from a hook and hurried back to me.

"How many rooms are there?" I asked, taking the keyring from her, fingering through it for the master.

"Twenty-four. He had plans drawn up for another…" Her voice trailed off. I was already at the first door.

We found the second finger in Room Fifteen and the third one in Room Twenty One. The first desecration had numbed us and we did little more than gasp with each successive mutilation. The note was in the last room we checked.

"Dear God," Susan whimpered. "He's written it in blood."

"He's gone to Gordon's Glen," I said, roughly grabbing her arm and turning her toward the door. "There's a lot of blood here. Marvin may still be alive. Let's go."

I knew that Steve would expect us to come up the main road, that he would be watching the entrance. But, only one other living person knew that property better than I. Only Frank would expect me to take the old wagon road and follow the river on foot to the homeplace.

"Where are you going?" Susan asked. "You missed the turn."

"We're going to surprise him and go in the back way."

The pickup nudged aside several saplings and climbed over numerous tree stumps, but it stalled at one of the narrow gorges that Sycamore Creek followed. We were close enough, though. I jumped out of the cab and began rummaging through the equipment in the back of the pickup. Somewhere in that truck bed, I knew that Marvin had a weapon.

"Here's a flashlight," Susan said, her voice sounding close in the darkness.

"I want a gun, Susan. We can't risk that light."

"I've already found a pistol," she said, distance invading her tone. "I tucked it in my waistband. There's a rifle over here. I felt the stock."

I felt my way around the pickup to her side and reached down to touch the comforting assurance of highly polished wood and clean metal. Why was the rifle out of its protective case?

"Shells," I mumbled. "Where's that light?"

Susan handed me the flashlight and I turned it on, confirming the last moment's suspicions. The rifle's chamber was empty. I threw the light around the bed of the pickup. There were no boxes of shells, no loose shells anywhere.

"Is that thing loaded?" I asked, flashing the light at the handgun poked in Susan's waistband. She gingerly lifted the pistol and handed it to me.

"Slimy bastard," I said, observing the empty cylinder.

"What can we do?" Susan asked. "He'll kill us, too."

"No chance," I said. "He won't know we're there until I'm close enough to strangle him."

I felt Susan shiver. Somehow, I had forgotten that Steve Benson was her brother. I had forgotten that he was human.

Chapter Thirty

By following the bank of Sycamore Creek, we reached the river rapids in just minutes. Before I saw the moon's reflection on the swift waters, I heard the hollow, sighing sound of water falling to the pool at the base of the waterfall.

"Watch your step," I cautioned. "The bank is crumbly along here and you could fall."

"Let me have your hand," Susan said. "You know where you're going. I don't."

I felt her cool hand slip into mine and we stood at the edge of the river, cool spray from the waterfall misting our faces. I stiffened when I heard the voices. Susan's hand grasped mine more tightly. Darkness lifted from around us and sunlight shone brightly on the two figures kneeling on the ground near the forest's edge, backs to us. A large, dark woman and a small, freckled boy. They had scooped a basketball-sized depression in the soft delta soil and I watched the woman place a dark object in the boy's hand. He clasped it tightly as he looked at her, a lightly disguised plea shadowing his large eyes. Then he looked over her shoulder and spied Susan and me.

"Hi," he said.

The woman turned and stared, her familiar black eyes warming. She smiled. I moved closer, pulling Susan along with me. Could it be? For a moment, I closed my eyes, remembering the words from years ago.

"See that man, son?" Mama Kate had told me, pointing to the strange couple standing by the waterfall. "Someday, you will be that man. Put all of your fear into the stone and bury it. That's good. Go on and shove the dirt over it. When you find the stone again, you will use the fear and it will no longer frighten you."

Slowly, I opened my eyes. The woman and boy were gone.

171

Darkness again surrounded us and I welcomed the waterfall's cool spray on my hot cheeks.

"Did you see them?" I asked.

"See *who*?"

I didn't answer. I thought I had left that particular dream on the mountainside. Part of me wondered if Kyanith would have seen the two if she, rather than Susan, had stood alongside me.

"It's not important," I told Susan, leading her down closer to the waterfall, toward the old river road. "Come on. It's less than half a mile from here to the house."

In the darkness, Susan and I both stumbled several times as we made our way up the rutted road and past the old cannery. At the fence marking the boundary between the peach orchard and the blackberry patch, I stopped and stood for a moment, leaning on a large cedar cornerpost.

"Something's not right," I told Susan.

"I know," she said, her voice low. "Shouldn't we be able to see lights from here?"

"Yeah. Lights in either the big house or the cottage would be visible."

"Maybe he's gone," Susan ventured.

"I doubt it. We would have heard the sound of his car engine. No, I have the feeling that Steve is in one of those houses."

"And Marvin, too."

"Yeah," I said, my throat tightening. "Marvin."

The moon, hidden for the last few minutes by a thin cloud, chose this moment to peek out and paint the buildings a ghostly white. I narrowed my eyes, seeking movement. Any movement.

"There's Steve's car," Susan said, pointing to a shadow between the cottage and the big house. "There! Underneath the oak tree!"

"It's moving!" I shouted. "He's coasting it down the hill. The bastard's outfoxed us again!"

"How did he know?" Susan cried.

"*Stop!*" I yelled, ignoring her question. "Steve Benson! Stop that car! Let Marvin go!"

Headlights came on and the car engine thundered to life. I ran toward the vehicle, knowing that I couldn't possibly stop it. Then, the car slowed.

"Cody, I have the sheriff. I'm going to the Violet Fern."

My knees buckled and I fell to the ground. Dust sifted into my nostrils and I choked at the earthy smell. I had not comprehended how powerful hate could be. I'd never felt this intensely about anything or anyone. Hot tears filled my eyes and spilled onto my cheeks. I raised myself to hands and knees and screamed at the departing car. A cry of frustration and rage. I'd make him pay. Steve Benson would suffer more than the combined total of all the pain he had ever caused. I would see to that.

*　*　*

Frank had left the keys in the ignition of Papa Gordon's old Willys Jeep. Rather than using the time to backtrack to Marvin's pickup down by the river, Susan and I had climbed into the jeep, hoping it had enough life and gasoline left to make it to the mine.

We didn't talk. The silence echoed our thoughts. By the time we reached the cutoff to the Violet Fern, my entire body was numb. Susan seemed frozen to the ragged upholstery of the passenger seat. She mumbled something.

"What did you say?" I asked. Susan cleared her throat.

"I just said that it was meant to be this way," she repeated. "We'll all be together up at the Violet Fern."

"Bull!"

"You can deny it all you want," Susan said. "But you have to admit that it's happening that way."

"Coincidence," I muttered. I didn't want to bring up the other possibility. Steve Benson had broken, that much we had witnessed. His hideous mutilation of Marvin had been only one superficial manifestation of his sickness. It was entirely feasible that he had taken this opportunity to seek revenge by destroying a whole group of people whom he saw as having hurt him.

"I don't think so," Susan said. I flinched. She had done it to me again: my thoughts must have been written in large, iridescent block letters.

"Give me another explanation."

"Look at it from this angle, Jackson. In the depths of his soul, Steve knew that he had to be at the Violet Fern at this time. Just as you did."

"I'm not sure that I believe that," I said, swerving to miss a large hole in the road. "Either part of it."

"I'm just assuming," Susan said. "Steve also knew that he had a confrontation due with you."

"He's known that for years," I said.

"Just listen. Steve knows that there will be a confrontation but, because he's never explored his soul, he doesn't know the type. He has to rely on his past experiences for reference."

"And I'm an expert?"

"I didn't say that, Jackson. But, you do know that the polarities have to be balanced."

"So you think that if I find some sort of equal and opposite emotion to balance his psychosis, then everything will be for the best and we'll all live happily ever after? Damn!"

I cursed as the right front wheel hit a sharp rock and the vehicle rolled toward the steep ditch. I jerked the steering wheel sharply left, but my move was too late and the old jeep wedged itself in the trench. Susan slammed forward and I heard a sickening thud as her forehead hit the solid metal dash.

"Susan!" I yelled, reaching for her shoulder. I felt movement underneath my hand.

"I'm okay, Jackson, but I'll have a black eye tomorrow."

She giggled dizzily and my heartbeat returned to its normal pace. I shifted into the lowest gear and gunned the engine. The jeep rocked a few inches and then settled back down into the tight space between the hillside and the road. Shifting into reverse, I tried vainly to back out.

"I could do it with a winch," I told Susan.

"But, we don't have one. And, we don't have time. Look up there ahead of us. At the top of the hill."

My eyes traveled past the dark pines, toward the clearing up above, and my throat tightened again. The blue light, familiar from the night before, shimmered in flamelike waves, tossing sparks hundreds of feet into the dark sky.

Chapter Thirty-One

"It's pulling us," Susan said, climbing out of the jeep and up the slope to the roadway. "Can't you feel it?"

I felt something, the source of which I was not sure, but it coincided with the pulsing of the magnetic light. It was as if the light itself were a living thing and, with each intake of its breath, we were being drawn closer. I stood, paralyzed, watching Susan's dark profile grow smaller as she trudged up the hill.

At that moment, I remembered that this was a dream—*my* dream— and I had control. The real me was back in Albuquerque, sleeping in the tiny trailer by the gasoline pumps. Or, perhaps the real me was in Missouri, dreaming the remainder of the night away after studying for college finals. Or, it could be that the real me was still five years old and had just drifted back into the dream that had been interrupted when Papa Gordon had told Mama about Elmer.

"Wait, Susan!" I yelled. With the iridescent light behind her, I could observe her expectant profile as she turned and waited for me. I was ready to get on with this dream and have it end.

"You have to use his hate, his anger," Susan said, when I fell into step beside her.

"Sure," I said, gasping for breath. "But, what about *my* hate and anger? I'm afraid that his emotions and mine both fall on the same end of the see-saw."

"You're right," she said slowly, seeming to search for words. "You both fall on the negative end. The polarities aren't balanced."

"No kidding."

"Don't be sarcastic, Jackson. This is serious. Can't you make your feelings positive?"

"Now, who's being sarcastic?"

"All feelings have positive and negative poles."

"I'm sorry, Susan. I feel only negative emotion toward Steve. Try as I might, I can't change that."

"Then we'll have to change Steve's feelings."

"Do you have any idea of the odds on being able to accomplish that little trick?"

"No," she said. I watched the blue light flicker over the pout on her face. "But, the others will have fresh ideas."

My pace quickened. I had almost forgotten about Kyanith and Frank. About Moonshadow and Dorrie. And, by now, Steve and Marvin would be with them at the Violet Fern.

"Do you suppose that they're still up at the mine?" I asked, sneaking a glance back over my shoulder. Susan's face glowed blue.

"They're there," she said. "There's no place else to go. Besides, it's already started."

"What has already started?"

"The metamorphosis," Susan said. She had caught up with me and looped her left arm through the bend in my right arm, pulling me along with her as she leaned forward.

"So, that's what you're calling it, now," I said, staring at the horizon. The blue light shifted in intensity, paling to a blue-white. Hot air rippled toward my body in almost perceptible waves.

"Look!" Susan cried. "The sparks! Like fireworks! Did you hear that scream? Kyanith?"

At that point, we both ran, unaware of the roots and rocks in the road, oblivious to the fact that we headed directly toward the danger. Kyanith's piercing scream faded away and a pervasive crackling sound filled the void. Susan made a gagging noise.

"I know," I said, slowing and gasping for breath. "It smells foul."

"Sulphur and brimstone," she said tonelessly. "We're headed for the gates of hell."

* * *

In the parking area above the tunnel, blue light reflected on and ran off of Steve Benson's luxury car. Susan and I stared at the car and then wordlessly inched over to the edge of the cliff above the tunnel. Like heat rising from a furnace, the blue light singed our faces as we stared at the scene below. Susan moaned and I put my arm around her shoulders, pulling her to me.

It's the worst kind of nightmare, I reminded myself, but I still have control. I control Steve Benson, crouched near the tunnel mouth, back against a thick ledge of quartz, shotgun pointed at a rigid Frank. *I*

176

control the situation. I control Kyanith, who has thrown her own body over an unconscious Dorrie. *I control the situation.* I control Moonshadow, who is wrapping a blanched and bloody Marvin's right hand with shreds of her long gypsy skirt. *I control the situation.*

I felt a tug as Susan slipped from my hold and began the descent down the stone steps. Her foot slipped on the third step and I watched her long fingers tear at the sparse vegetation on the steep hillside before she caught hold and righted her body.

As if from a great distance, and in another space, I watched the beings down below. Like so many tiny insect workers, they scurried about their tasks, each seemingly oblivious to his relative unimportance. Or, to his *importance*, a voice within nagged. In that moment, I knew that we are both more and less than we think we are. Like sound and light, we stretch out from either side of that which is visible or audible. We form an infinite spectrum, realizing only a tiny portion of our totality.

And, just as quickly, I again became an undeniable part of the group I had watched. This play could not continue without my participation. Shielding my face from the penetrating blue light, I began the descent down the steep stone steps.

Chapter Thirty-Two

"I'm going to kill you, Jackson," Steve said, eyes blazing yellow madness. "But I'll see that you take a long time to die."

"That's a bad line from a B-grade western," I told him, looking at the circle of white, expectant faces around me. Each harboured hope that I was the catalyst, the means by which this ugly alliance would be cemented. I turned back to the man who faced me, mottled face reflecting purple.

"These people are no good to you, Benson," I cajoled. "It's me that you really want to hurt. Let them go."

"No," he whispered, madness permeating his tone. "These people are the means to make you suffer. You want to know how? Watch!"

The barrel of his weapon swung left, around to Frank, and paused. I watched his finger tighten on the trigger.

"No!" I screamed, rushing toward him. In slow motion, I saw Steve's finger flinch and, almost instantly, Frank dropped to his knees, fingers of his left hand loosely clutching a ragged hole that bloodied his right shoulder. I grabbed for the barrel of the shotgun and felt the heat from the metal before Steve turned it on Susan. Calmly, he looked at me and smiled. His eyes held no more humanity than those of a mad dog.

"She's next," he said, lowering the barrel to a spot below Susan's waist. "Her and that bastard girl of hers."

He shifted the shotgun's sights to Kyanith. She stared at him defiantly, her face rigid.

"Susan thought I didn't know," he said, looking at me. His thin lips splayed across his porcelain teeth. "But I found out. Whore!" he screamed, swinging the barrel back to Susan. "Slut!"

Susan stood, unmoving, hands dangling limply at her sides. The look turned on her brother conveyed both horror and disgust.

"Use it, Jackson," the voice came from behind me. "Use his anger!"

"Shut up, you goddamned witch!" Steve shouted, turning on Moonshadow. The shotgun barrel tilted slightly toward the ground. I made two steps and grabbed. But, I hadn't counted on the madman's strength. He pulled away from me, still holding the stock of the gun, finger still wrapped around the trigger.

"Think of love," Moonshadow screamed. "Good memories!"

"Not one of them will die quickly," Steve said. He was so close that I felt the heat of his words on my face, the poison of his spittle. He grinned again and swung the shotgun, trying to shake me off. I held on tightly, trying to re-form my thoughts. Attempting to think of anything other than the depths to which I despised this man.

"You're going the wrong way, Jackson. Move to the other end!"

It was Kyanith's voice. She had picked up on my hatred. Then the struggle ceased. The blue light was gone and I stood alone in a desert wasteland. I heard voices and moved toward the sound.

"Jackson?"

I recognized Susan's voice and followed it, picking my way over a stack of something that resembled human bones. She appeared, a darker shadow in the night, and I reached for her.

"Don't touch me," she whispered, moving away. "I'm contaminated."

"Contaminated?"

"We all are," she said. "I don't know how you escaped."

"What caused it?" I asked.

"Pollution," she said. "Radioactive waste. War."

"I don't understand."

"Jackson, we humans have ruined earth! We can't even see the sun!"

"Naturally, we can't," I said, moving closer, trying to discern her face. "It's night."

"This is not a normal darkness," Susan protested. "I saw the sun about a year ago. That was the last time. You're now standing in a dried-up river bed. Our water is almost gone."

"Tell me what caused this!"

"We had a chance," she said, wistfully. "I don't even remember what it was, or when. But, we didn't try. We didn't do what had to be done."

She turned her face as a dim light appeared from somewhere nearby. Horrified, I stared at the hole where her nose should have been, the crusty strings that dripped from her pus-filled eyes. She raised both

179

hands in front of her face.

"Go away, Jackson. Save yourself. For the rest of us, it's too late."

"It's too late. Too late. too late…"

The words echoed in my ears. I strained the fibers in my body to their maximum as I struggled to pull the shotgun from Steve. I raised my eyes to his face and felt my body grow weak as I stared into his eyes.

"I've won!" Steve shouted. An almost disbelieving smile lifted the corners of his drooling mouth. He licked his lips and pulled the barrel of the gun from my limber grasp. I watched the confidence flow into his limbs as he stood erect. Surety of his success blazed in fiery streamers from his eyes.

"Dear God, no!" Kyanith screamed. "You're our only chance, Jackson. Help us!"

I felt my bladder lose control and warm liquid seeped down the inner thighs of both my legs. I fell to my knees. Years ago, Mama Kate and I had discussed it. The fear. My worst enemy. The extreme emotion. Warm, foul-smelling liquid drenched my head and face, and I raised my head when Steve Benson laughed.

"I'll piss on them, too, Jackson. All of them. And, you'll watch."

"Jackson." Kyanith whimpered. "Please…"

I had done it. I had let them all down. We had lost. I was lost. The pyramid from my childhood dreams nestled down on my shoulders, covering my head. I struggled to breathe. The whistling began, piercingly sharp, threatening to shatter my eardrums. It increased in intensity and then dropped abruptly, growing into the sweetest sound I'd ever heard.

I opened my eyes and the blue light was gone. A dark mass on the ground took shape and I recognized Steve Benson. The glorious music continued, a hundred symphonies in harmony. I'd never heard anything so beautiful.

"You did it, Jackson."

Thin arms looped around my neck and I raised myself to my knees, holding Kyanith tightly. *What* did I do? Where were the others?

"I felt your fear and his assuredness," she said. "I aligned myself with your fear to give it more strength."

"Yeah," I said weakly. "We were on the wrong path, still thinking in terms of good and bad."

"Steve was full of hate, which we all considered negative," Kyanith said. "And you were capable of much love, which we considered positive. Love and hate. And yet the seperation of the two is caused by fear. Fear was the *real* emotion involved, the overlying factor we almost missed."

"Kyanith," I interrupted her. "Where are the others?"

"Everyone will be fine, Jackson. The others are temporarily asleep, but they'll waken soon. Do you hear it?"

"The music?" I asked. "Yes. It's beautiful. Where is it coming from?"

"The beings," Kyanith said, placing her hand on my cheek and turning my head toward the tunnel. "You've freed them."

"The birds?" I asked, feeling, rather than seeing, the vibratory flutter as thousands of wings soared past me.

"You remember them, now, don't you?"

"I think so," I said. "We each had seventeen stripes on each wing. Folded by our sides, in our sleeping units, they formed perfect chevrons if seen from above. But Kyanith, where will they go now?"

"Everywhere," Kyanith said. "Nowhere."

"What was our purpose in freeing them?"

"You forget, Jackson, that you've always had an open channel to your creator, your maker, your highest self. At times, *you* chose to close the door, to ignore advice and guidance. But, the world is populated with thousands of people who have *never* had that opportunity. They were manifested by our crew and, for thousands of years, have been cut off from their source, their inner connectedness, that vitality from which they sprang."

"I've heard that before. Those same words."

"We each have," Kyanith said. "Never did our highest selves let us forget our assignments. And our duties."

"It's over?"

"This phase is over, Jackson. You can rest, now."

Epilogue

It happened three years ago, today. There are times when I think of it and it was yesterday's nightmare. At other times, it didn't happen. And, during still other moments, I think that it happened, but it happened to someone other than myself.

Except for Kyanith, we're all still here near Bethel Bluff. Susan and I moved into the big house here at Gordon's Glen. After three years of remodeling and rebuilding, the house looks almost as it did when I grew up here. We've modified somewhat by adding solar collectors; the river generates our energy and we are almost energy self-sufficient.

I've taken over Papa Gordon's library as my office and I'm writing again. Just yesterday, I received a call from my agent. He likes my latest novel, a story of returning home, and a large motion picture studio is very interested in a screenplay.

Now that she has free time, Susan thinks that she may initiate a guild for the ladies of the community who work with their hands, making crafts. She wants to find some use for Benson's Inn, which has been boarded up and closed since we returned from the mine. She says that the structure is ideal for the intended purposes: it is close to the highway, has excellent parking, and there are separate spaces for all vendors. And, as she reminds me, we can use the token revenue for Steve's care.

Steve has become a permanent resident in a private nursing home near Little Rock. When daylight arrived that morning, his injuries had been the most severe of any. By the time we got him down the mountain and to the emergency room in a Hot Springs hospital, he had been comatose: he has never regained consciousness. The doctors tell us that there is no medical reason for his state, that even the trauma accompanying sudden blindness shouldn't have produced such drastic results.

Marvin resigned from the sheriff's department almost immediately. He and Tillie bought the old bait shop out by Hedges Crossing and operating the business in the summer keeps them busy enough to appreciate the winter slack. Marvin's right hand has healed remarkably well and, with his thumb and little finger, he can still do anything as well as any man I know. I'm thankful that Steve didn't remember that Marvin is a natural southpaw.

Dorrie Jacobs married Tommy Waite, the young man who replaced Marvin in the Sheriff's Department, last year. She and Tommy are extremely happy and expecting their first child any day. Susan and I have discussed how to funnel Steve's sizeable holdings to the child without Dorrie knowing. After all, Steve is the child's grandfather.

Frank and Moonshadow have expanded the guest cottage, adding a large living area and another bedroom. Using Moonshadow's money, they hired two California experts, tore out the peach and apple orchards, and replanted the area with grapevines. With a certain amount of modifications, the old cannery and warehouses will house their winery. I watch the two of them together and sometimes wonder whether Frank has changed his sexual preferences. Then I listen to Moonshadow and become realistic. Living with her, I, too, would remain gay.

I haven't seen Kyanith for three years. Not since the moment it was over and she told me I could rest. Before I had fallen into a trance-like sleep, I had watched her walk to the tunnel entrance and stand. When my vision had grown fuzzy, I had imagined I saw a ripply white light materializing around her, slowly spinning in a clockwise direction. Although Susan has insisted that Kyanith came to her and explained the reasons for her departure, she won't tell me.

We've all gathered together a couple of times and discussed those hours. Nobody seems too sure of what happened in and around the tunnel. Frank, Marvin, and I went back a week later and we couldn't find the tunnel. It was as if it had never been there. At the base of the pit, where we remembered the tunnel being, a broad, six-foot-high bank of solid quartz stretched for almost two hundred yards.

We don't discuss the mysticism surrounding the event. I suppose that each of us has internalized something of the happening and the premise surrounding it. I think that we are greater, yet humbler, for the experience. I feel more compassion and, at the same time, contradictory though it might sound, I feel less attachment to societal demands. I now know that I am part of something greater and I chose this life to understand and nourish an aspect that the greater part of myself had not the capabilities to experience.

Each of us has had the opportunity to exercise the lesson of good/bad and positive/negative. Life has become simpler since I have realized that I need feel no guilt for my emotions. If there is no guilt, there is no fear of recrimination. When there is no fear, there can only be light.

I find myself wondering why, after almost three years, I should pick up these faded pages and attempt some sort of culmination. The sensible side of me knows that this manuscript is not the sort of writing that a book company would wish to publish, that I would never seek to have it published. But, the mystical side of me knows the reason, realizes why it must be available for reading and study. The reminder came this morning.

*   *   *

I went back to the Violet Fern today. Before dawn, I had awakened with a nagging sense of urgency, a feeling that I couldn't attach to any of my current projects. Moving carefully, so as not to disturb Susan, I had slipped out of bed and gone to the east window. Standing there, feeling the night breeze move the soft curtains against my face, I watched star after star slip into oblivion as the advance light from the sun grayed the sky.

I can't see them, I thought, so those stars no longer exist. Amusement and nostalgia for my naivete of three years ago washed over me. Because I hadn't been constantly immersed in studying my spiritual progress, I had not, until that moment, fully comprehended the great strides that I had taken, the enormous changes in my thinking processes.

I can't say when my thoughts changed; I can't describe how they changed; I can't even measure the extent of change. I simply know that I now accept any possibility. The boundaries that defined my mind have grown hazy at the edges. I realize that there are only possibilities. But, implied in that statement is the answer: Even impossibility is a possibility.

So, perhaps everything that I've reported—and even more—was possible during those intense hours at the Violet Fern three years ago. Even if it had been only a dream, I had experienced it, had given it energy, and had, therefore, caused it to come into being. It is an undeniable part of me.

I would like to yell and shout about the growth steps I've taken. I would like to show people how much more I am than I was formerly. But, assuming that I could find someone who would listen, how could I illustrate the example? The listener would have no comprehension of the person I was before. It was at that moment, the moment the sun had peeked a small sliver over the eastern horizon, that I knew I would find the answer at the Violet Fern.

* * *

The new four wheel drive pickup that Frank had bought possessed neither the stamina of Marvin's old yellow pickup nor the tenacity of Papa Gordon's old Willys Jeep but, with proper coaxing and maximum patience, I drove it all the way to the parking area above the open pit.

Heat simmered in wavy lines from the red clay and white boulders. After the air-conditioned pickup cab, the hot, moist air fell around me like a thick towel dampened in hot water. I stared at the open pit for a few minutes, observing that the loose earth on all sides had gravitated toward the bottom and the gaping wound was slowly being healed.

I turned then, because I had not come to see the mine. I wanted to find one spot between the mine and the cabin. A special place beside the trail where I had sat on a stump and had met a probable self—one who had walked through a rainbow.

Sawbriers had grown in from both sides of the trail, making it impossible in some areas to follow the faint track, forcing me to step off and tread through thick underbrush. It was on one of these detours that I saw the young man leaning against an oak tree, right foot propped on a decaying log.

"Don't come any closer!" he shouted. "I have a gun!"

"Hold it, son," I said, freezing in the spot and holding out my bare hands. "I've no weapon. I'm not going to hurt you."

"Don't move," he ordered, lifting his right foot off the log and stepping toward me. I observed the rifle he carried, a clean, slick Marlin 30-30. A deer rifle.

"Son, we can't have any poaching on this land," I told him, slowly dropping my hands to waist level. "Plus, you're out of season to be hunting."

He screwed his face in anger and I was reminded of someone. My mind raced, flashing pictures of all the young men in Bethel Bluff, but I couldn't place this young rebel.

"You can't tell me what I can or can't do on my own property," he gritted. "Unless you're a game warden."

His own property. I squinted my eyes, bringing his face into sharp focus. In amazement, I stared at the wide-set hazel eyes, the light sprinkling of freckles across the straight nose, the deep scar in his chin. Short, uneven strands of chestnut hair peeked out from underneath the edges of his brown baseball cap.

"I'm not a warden," I told him. "I'm someone who used to live around here. I just thought I'd walk around here and see how things have changed."

I watched his shoulders drop as he relaxed. The barrel of the rifle pointed toward the ground.

"I thought you looked familiar," he said, sitting down on the log and propping the rifle near him. He frowned up at me. "Are you a friend of Papa Gordon's?"

I nodded, wishing that there was some way I could tell this young man who he was, what he would do and that, in twenty-five years or so, he would be here, only *he* would be the one who was standing and talking to his younger self. *But, would that be the case?*

Am I a probable self of this young man, I asked myself, or am I a future self? And, then it was there. The answer. The incident I'd blocked from my mind for so many years.

"What's your name?" he asked, and the question harmonized with the question from my memory. I paused, considering my answer.

"I'm called Etal," I said. Again, the answer made a perfect tone to memory's answer.

"Is that your first name? Or, your last?"

"Just Etal," I said. "Gordon will remember me."

As a teen, I had turned to pick up my rifle and, when I had looked up, the old man had been gone. As a teen, I had forgotten the incident and had never asked Papa Gordon about a man named Etal. Would this younger me remember? Would he remember what I had forgotten?

In slow motion, I watched his head turn and observed the childish curve of his cheek. God, I loved that young man, full of optimism and hope, bubbling with creativity and vulnerability. Suddenly I knew that I wanted to be a future self, rather than a probable self, of this young man. At the point in his life at which I am now, I wanted him to look back and experience the agape, the unconditional love, for himself that I felt at this moment. And, at that time, I knew it would be so.

Overhead, thunder rolled deeply and I looked up at the dark underside of a heavy thundercloud. When my gaze returned to the fallen log, the boy was gone. I felt the stiff muscles of my cheeks crack in a relieved smile. Then I paused, remembering something else. Rushing over to the fallen log, I dropped to my hands and knees and patted the dry leaves.

It has to be here, I thought, sifting the crumbly leaves through the openings between my fingers. I raked at the earth, feeling my finger-nails pull back into the quick. The Jackson I had been the day that I met the old man in the woods had lost the item by that fallen log.

My heartbeat slowed to normal when I touched the cool, slick sides. The fear stone, young Jackson had called it, having dug it up a couple of years prior to the encounter. Now, I sat back on my haunches and carefully observed the stone. It was a dark blue, rather than black, and its translucency allowed just enough light to pass through so that the blue appeared to constantly change hues. The side turned up had a crude, five pointed star scratched on the surface. Knowing that the opposite surface had my name carved in it, I slipped it down into my jeans' pocket and began the trek back uphill to Frank's pickup. Thunder growled and I heard the sizzle of lightning as it passed not far from my path.

I was halfway down the mountain before I made the connection and laughed aloud. An old man. Even though I was only forty-five, the young Jackson had seen an old man. I had grown accustomed to seeing my face in the mirror. It had taken awhile, but now I expected the gray-streaked hair, the deep wrinkles, the rounded shoulders. Physically, I had aged twenty years during that initial encounter at the Violet Fern with Kyanith. Most surely, there was a probable me in another reality who had not undergone such drastic change.

It would be good to get home. I understood that, in this life, our responsibilities at the Violet Fern were over. But first, I knew that there was something that had to be done.

Frank's pickup didn't make it as far as Marvin's had on that memorable night years ago, but it was only a short hike to the waterfall. When I reached the clearing, I paused for a breath, orienting myself before I made for the edge of the forest.

The soft soil scooped easily and I had dug a hole almost a foot deep before I stopped and laid the stone in the hole. I gasped when I read the carved name, *Etal*. For almost forty years, I had been positive that the name carved on the rock had been *Jackson*. I shrugged and crumbled some loose dirt over the bluish black stone.

I knew now that there would never be anyone whom I could tell of my growth, my experiences, my successes. There had been only one possibility, one person who could have understood, and I had chosen to leave things as they were. Or, had *he* chosen to reject the probability?

I sifted the dirt over the stone, making a smooth, loosely packed mound. Pressing the center of the mound, I packed the dirt. It must be buried correctly in order for the past Kyanith to find it at the right time. Then I raised myself to my feet, savoring the earthy smell of the soil on my hands, treasuring the sound of the wind rustling through the tall pines, relishing the cool spray from the waterfall as it misted my face.

Brushing the black soil from my hands, I turned toward Gordon's Glen. I found myself thinking of the probability that might have been if I had remembered the exact name carved on the stone.

The End

THE CRYSTAL SPIRAL
by
T.K. Lebeau

... Amanda reached over and grabbed my hand. I felt the coldness of her flesh. Her intensity charged through me like an electric current.

"We can't let anyone else get to the ruins, Branch. Nobody else must be near. Henry's soul depends on it!"

As I opened the car door and stepped out, I thought about her words. Not Henry's *life*. Henry's *soul*. I felt beads of perspiration on my forehead and upper lip. The cool night air turned my skin clammy.

Darkness surrounded me when I stumbled behind her as she sure-footedly climbed the trail. Then she was gone. In the dim light, I searched for a clue, some kind of opening through which she had gone. I found nothing.

From *The Crystal Spiral*
by T. K. Lebeau, Volume III of the Crystal Soul Merge Series